PIERRE KROFT PRESTIGE LEGACY PUBLISHERS
4075 Jefferson Parkway
Lake Oswego, Oregon 97035
United States
Copyright 2022 Christian Filostrat
Publication date February 2024

Library of Congress Cataloguing-in-Publication Data
Filostrat, Christian
Until you, who? / Christian Filostrat
p. cm
1. Zaire – DRC – Belgian Congo – Angola – Leopold II – Mobutu Sese Seko History. 2. Belgium – Colonies – History – Blacks – Race identity. 6. Cultural assimilation. I. Title

"Like all Europeans," Father Brabant declared, "you're having a first-day-in-Africa letdown." That will fade as soon as you become acclimated to the Congo. Your minds will adjust, not because the Congo has changed, but because you have embraced the opportunities to change the place. And you'll thank God for these opportunities, and you'll grow even more sympathetic to the Congo; you'll become champions of your captives. "You see," he continued, "things are out of place in Leopoldville's Bantu sector; the people you're passing through here belong in a forest or village somewhere out there, not in a city." You're witnessing the agony of a village giving birth to a city. Such origins are always agonizing. It was said to be agonizing in Europe during the Middle Ages. It's startling in Africa."

Pierre Kroft Prestige Legacy Publishers
Until you, who? A love Story

About the author

A 1994 Presidential Award recipient, Christian Filostrat is a senior American diplomat and a National War College alumnus. From the Bronx, New York, Christian Filostrat has a PhD in international affairs and is the author of <u>The Secret of the Dictator</u>, a novel about the political dynamics between the United States and the Democratic Republic of the Congo. The first book in his Congo trilogy, <u>Containing China</u>, tells the story of an American meddling in a Congolese cardinal's papal election. <u>Until You, Who</u>, the final book in the trilogy, tells the story of the Catholic Church in the Congo following World War II.

Christian Filostrat's scholarly study <u>Négritude and its Revolution</u> is based on the publication L'Etudiant Noir and Aimé Césaire's article <u>Racial Consciousness and Social Revolution</u>, which launched the Négritude movement in Paris in 1935.

The best-selling <u>Frantz Fanon in the United States</u>: With the help of Frantz Fanon's devoted wife Josie, the author has the privilege of visiting the revolutionary Frantz Fanon on his death bed. In this intimate encounter, Fanon passionately shares his unwavering dedication to the Algerian Revolution. An extraordinary work about the revolutionary who lives in legend.

2024
PIERRE KROFT PRESTIGE LEGACY PUBLISHERS
DISTRIBUTION CONTROLLED BY PIERRE KROFT
BOOK DISTRIBUTOR

Until you, who?
A love story
by
Christian Filostrat

Until you, who?
A love story

FOREWORD

Whenever I'm on a flight, I engage in conversations with the people seated beside me. That helps me with my fear of flying and advances the clock. In October 1999, I had a memorable encounter with a nun who happened to be seated next to me during a flight from Kinshasa to Brussels. Her story captivated me instantly, her passion for sharing it evident. I paid close attention to what she said about the infection that was by then known as HIV/AIDS. She was certain she had dealt with it when she worked as a nurse in Wembo-Nyama, situated in Sunkuru Province in the middle of the Democratic Republic of the Congo back in the 1950s.

I couldn't help but notice her deep sadness over the ongoing conflict in the Congo. She viewed the country as being stuck in an endless cycle of despair with no way out. She had a keen eye for detail and provided a perceptive analysis.

Sister Immanuel is eager to share the story of her life's journey, as she has devoted 54 years to nursing in the Congo. However, the majority of the information she shared with me revolved around Mària. Or as she put it "the love of my life's story."

She also grapples with the constant shadow of suicide. A recurring problem that never fails to catch you off guard. After learning about her mother's tragic death on the day she made her solemn vows, she was left pondering a deep question: "Can one truly exist when there is no purpose to existence?" Both her uncle and her beloved followed suit. There were more.

Alone, she bears witness to the Congo's journey towards independence. She arrived in 1945 and now has a front row seat. She meticulously describes the actions of the Congolese people and Belgium's maneuvers to maintain control over a colony marked by suffering. She confronts the question of suicide by vividly painting a picture of her own demise.

Chapter 1

Ever since Jerome, my loyal house servant, handed them to me during the ceremony where I was appointed as head nurse of the Wembo-Nyama hospital in the Congo on December 12, 1949, these pillows have been an absolute godsend. Jerome dedicated more than a year to gathering down feathers from elusive Cameroon Scrub-Warbler nests and crafting pillows from two lion skins acquired at the Leopoldville Central Market. He stored them in his room, patiently biding his time to present them to me. They are the world's two most comfortable pillows.

When I returned to Tournai, my hometown in southwest Belgium that I had left fifty-four years before, I was accompanied by Jerome and the pillows that had journeyed with me for over half a century. I've cherished them both more than any other gift.

Resting on Jerome's pillows, I release my longing to connect with the world beyond the walls of Maison St Jean, the nursing home in Tournai. Here, I believe I possess a tale that is truly one-of-a-kind — a tale that is not self-centered, biased, or a mere figment of imagination. Despite what others have told me to my face, this is not the story of an elderly nun. I prefer the term "renunciant," as "nun" has only recently become a term used to address an aged woman confined to a cloister, weaving her regrets and self-absorption into a quest for redemption from a life that feels wasted and unnatural.

Of course, in the grand scheme of time, it's not an exceptional story; but it is – where it counts – in the tale of two simple renunciants. When people read a significant story, they do not recognize it. Even more so, if it's a story about a nun celebrating her own existence. I wish people had the patience of my notebook, which can handle anything with a patient smile. Or, as young Anne Frank put it, "*Papier heeft meer geduld dan mensen;*" and it's true: 'paper has more patience than people.'

In Maison St. Jean, I write about Mària and me for an hour in the morning, and if I can find a moment of genuine introspection before 3 p.m., undisturbed by the persistent presence in my mind, I carry on writing for another ninety minutes in the afternoon. I ponder silently, contemplating the words I should write and the extent to which I should express myself. I constantly remind myself of the sacred duty of confidentiality, a solemn vow to never disclose anything that may bring harm to my order. I feel the constant struggle between my inner turmoil and the burning desire to share my life experiences.

Kathryn Hulme's The Nun's Story, a 1956 novel, offers a profound exploration of the daily life of a nun. It takes readers on a journey from her initial aspirations to the momentous occasion of her final vows and beyond. The story traces the path of a Belgian nun, from her entrance into the convent to her departure into a world ravaged by war. This book stands out as a true masterpiece among the countless others I've read. After reading *The Nun's Story*, I feel more comfortable discussing my experiences as a nun. The journey that Ms.

Hulme describes is so detailed that when I read *The Nun's Story* in one night, it transported me back to the depths of Priscilla's Catacombs, the intricate tunnels beneath Rome, and the awe-inspiring Basilica of San Silvestro that I had the privilege of visiting in 1964.

In Ms. Hulme's story, even the nun's undergarments are brought into discussion. And, naturally, it's all about the Rules that must be adhered to, meticulously detailed and endlessly debated. I always keep *The Nun's Story* by my bedside, reading it over and over again as if it were my personal journal. It's much simpler to discuss others rather than oneself. Obsession with facts can consume those who observe from a distance or experience life vicariously through others. When the desire is intense, an individual must be discerning, careful, and even cunning, especially if a beloved is involved. What more is there to be said? Oddly enough, discussing Mària somehow eases the burden of discussing myself. Luckily, Ms. Hulme's novel is rich in the nun's self-denial and the convent's cunning strategy to deceive life, or "her life against nature," as Ms. Hulme aptly describes it. That has given me the opening I needed to tell Mària's and my story without getting bogged down in the details of a nun's convent daily life and compromising our sacred vows.

I figure that since Ms Hulme has already covered everything there is to know about a Belgian nun's daily routine in meticulous precision and more beautifully than I could ever do, I find myself inclined to take a different approach. I can be perverse — not contrarian — about revealing the indulgences

Mària and I didn't deny ourselves out of shame, arrogance, or delight, and don't forget the inescapable fact of old age. I can flip Ms. Hulme's Nun's Story upside down by recounting the tales of two nuns who defied the Rules to embrace their true selves.

Now, with no need to fret over uttering inappropriate words, my attention is directed towards the sacred bond between Mària and myself, rather than the bond of sisterhood. Thanks to Ms. Hulme's novel, our story can now focus on crafting a journey filled with personal accounts from an insider's perspective. It aims to evoke both knowing smiles from women and frowns from prelates, or perhaps even both, from anyone who takes an interest in our story. Yet I do not deceive myself. It's hard to convince anyone, especially those men who talk about women without understanding them. I can't help but be concerned that recounting the tale of two youthful nuns engaging in euphoric intimacy, reminiscent of the artistic flair of Gertrude Stein and Alice B. Toklas, may face certain restrictions. Yet the relentless urge to forge connections with the world beyond persists, unyielding, despite the inescapable truth of my age.

I fear for my health, dreading the day when I may become dependent on the staff, who, instead of addressing me as Sister Immanuel, mockingly refer to me as "La Folle de Tournai." I'd rather not have to rely on others for help. (The name was inspired by their discovery of the play La Folle de Chaillot by Jean Giraudoux.) They whisper about it when I'm not around, consumed by thoughts of the inheritance they anticipate from my estate. But things could be different next week. However, I remain vigilant. I'm not stupidly waiting to croak.

My biggest fear is that I won't do justice to my beloved, or that I'll be overly talkative and create a clunky portrayal of someone who isn't a saint. Or that I won't tell the love story of my life as it should be told

Father Brabant told us that Heaven looks kindly on love; I'm sure it doesn't look kindly on dishonest nuns.

Every note I've kept about Mària and me since fourth grade is woven together by the haunting presence of suicide. The word "Suicide" echoes persistently in my mind, relentlessly challenging me: "What can one do when life loses its meaning, ugh?" Suicide is a tumultuous word. It haunts my sleepless nights, murmuring life's greatest enigma in my mind. Then, for weeks, like a sudden hush after a storm, Suicide goes quiet without any explanation, leaving me feeling uneasy as I await its inevitable comeback to haunt me with its relentless question about the value of life.

Back in 1964, a neurologist at the Catholic Hospital Salvator Mundi in Rome gave me a diagnosis of tinnitus. He referred to it as the "lonely ailment" since I was the only one who could hear its sound. There are many different factors that can contribute to tinnitus, but one common cause is when the brain misinterprets sound, resulting in the perception of ringing or buzzing. He thought the suicide voice I was hearing was precipitated by a hormonal shift since I became a nun. There was no cure, and he advised me to renounce my vows before I killed myself.

Ever since my aunt delivered the news about my mother's tragic death, suicide has become a constant companion, always looming with its somber and brooding presence. I was just a child of 11 when she passed away, but it wasn't until twelve years later, on the day I embraced a life of renunciation as a nun, that I finally learned the truth.

On the morning of August 17, 1945, a somber atmosphere loomed over the town as the overcast sky and chilly air created a wintry scene. The smoke from the chimneys only added to the gloom, making the day even more surly. I solemnly made the formal vows just an hour ago, followed by the humble vows of a Perpetual Cross renunciant.

Mària has been by my side since fourth grade, her unique Garbo-li features concealed by her wimple. The Perpetual Cross garment she wears distinguishes her from the members of other orders, covering her hair and encircling her neck and chin.

Having achieved her goal of becoming a nun, she exudes joy. With her unwavering commitment to Almighty God before the Virgin Mary, heaven, and the crowds of people crammed inside our magnificent 13th century gothic Cathedral of Notre Dame de Tournai,* she radiates with a celestial beauty that captivates all who behold her like a Peter Paul Ruben angel. Each of us, as new renunciants, is touched by the radiance of Mària's spirit.

*Tournai is a city in western Belgium, near the French border. It's known for the huge Cathedral of Notre-Dame, with 5 towers and a rose window.

Marching with a sense of solemnity in a ceremonial procession, and singing with heartfelt passion the *Veni Creator Spiritu*, we exit the cathedral to receive congratulations and well-wishes from the whole world, pleased for us and relieved that the war has come to an end. The dirty ones The Germans have departed from Belgium. Mària gently tightens her grip on my hand as we come across a gathering of women with shaved heads, unmistakably collaborators, all clad in somber black, positioned off to the left, distanced from the center. She won't squeeze my hand again that day.

Alongside the women collaborators, there are two African families who have united, possibly seeking a sense of belonging. They are like outcasts who find protection in the company of other outcasts.

After the procession ended, we found comfort in the embrace of our loved ones. My aunt positioned herself outside, to the right of the main entrance, in order to keep an eye on me. She grabbed onto my habit's sleeve and tugged with all her might. She is a small woman. After my mother passed away, I've come to understand the reason behind her preference for wearing black. Her complexion has a muted yellow hue, accompanied by an unsettling expression.

I'm holding Mària's left hand in my right. However, my aunt, whom I refer to as Tantie, insists on having a private conversation with me. She mentioned that it's something of a personal nature. Mària suddenly releases my hand, and I feel a sudden pang in my heart caused by Mària's abrupt withdrawal.

My aunt delivers a statement on the steps of Notre Dame de Tournai on this chilly Lord's Day of my vows in August 1945. "Today you can know that your mother didn't die of typhoid as your father told you," according to her. "She ended her own life. Only your innocence and prayers can rescue her at this point. Because God is generous, He has entrusted that responsibility to you. Numb and like a figure in an old cartoon I look left and right.

After lunch, which I don't eat, she has my uncle drive me across the border into France to the village of Forest-sur-Marque, where my mother hanged herself. This is also where my mother taught second grade.

The tree remains, looking injured or offended in some way, forlorn as an alien, lost against the overcast span of the frayed sky on the outskirts of a park named after Marshal Petain. I approach it as if it were the Cross, then kneel to pray to an Icon. This park will forever serve as a clandestine memorial to my mother's end

After I had looked at the tree for a long time and wondered why she had picked it, my uncle, whom I call Tonton, pointed out that he had cut the branch. And, using hand signals to avoid disturbing the reverent silence and sporadic wind, he explains that he amputated the tree at my aunt's request and was fined ten thousand francs by the Forest-sur-Marque gendarmerie, which looked askance at the desecration of a park bearing the marshal's name. I wish Mària were here to tell me what to think, but I couldn't tell her my mother had committed suicide.

To break the silence while we were driving back to Tournai, my uncle said to me, "No one was certain what led your mother to do what she did back in 1934." While he said this, he looked straight ahead. "When I think back on it, I can still vividly recall how upset your mother was over your father leaving with that cousin from Lille. He was a wild womanizer." After that, my uncle starts yelling at me. "The incarnation of a goat if there ever was one. He came up with the idea of telling you that your mother had died of typhoid fever."

I remember my mother being bedridden off and on for a long time, as long as long is for a child of twelve. The physician whose name escapes me but I believe it was Lubin came to see her every evening, mumbling that her immune system was in dreadful shape, using the term "out of wack" to describe her immune system. But he didn't seem sure. He suggested that my mother get rid of our two cats. It was a suggestion, a wild guess, he said. He wasn't sure. He had seen a similar case in Brussels where the family there also had cats. He discussed her condition with my uncle, a gynecologist, explaining that he didn't understand why the front lobe of my mother's brain seemed infected as if by a virus, causing the headaches, sore lymph nodes and pains in her limbs' muscles. (Virology was a new science.) He wasn't sure. He palpated my mother's breasts a lot to ascertain her condition. He was seeking a cause. It could be in her breast. The day she died, she seemed much better, however; drove me to school in the morning with no deviation from the way she always behaved on her way to Forest-sur-Marque in the little Simca car we nicknamed "Plume" after my favorite cat that had died the year before. (We loved that cat so much we had it cremated and put the ashes on a shelf with a vase of flowers in my room.) I don't remember my father being there. Sixty-six years after my mother died, I read in *The Acta Clinica Belgica* medical journal about suicides caused by degeneration of frontal lobes from toxoplasmosis. Had my mother really been infected by our cats with toxoplasmosis?

"Had she had a firearm, I'm sure she'd have used it. It's simpler," my uncle adds offhandedly. "But perhaps she wouldn't have wanted to impose more inconvenience on us. She was a very considerate person, your mother was. But thank God she was found.

"There's one thing I'm certain of: being is intolerable if it's all you've got. It's not how to stay alive that's the mystery of life, but how to find something to live for. It's not enough to know that the sun will rise again tomorrow."

But I was hers. She didn't care about me that much? I'd like to know. In my head, I said it. All of it was in my head, just like the strange drumbeat questioning me about life's worth I heard while my uncle and I were pulling out of the driveway earlier.

The rain has already resumed by that time. Is there a breeze? The rain refuses to let the breeze through. People in Tournai, pray for droughts.

My uncle settles back into his customary silence, to let me unravel by myself the meaning of my mother's suicide. Perhaps because he knows how much the rain comforts me, he thinks the drizzle will do more to ease my bewilderment. It's up to me to make sense of the day's revelations.

In my aunt's eyes, my mother committed *the* sin. Whether she could not bear being alive because that's all her life had, she committed *the* sin. She needed no less than a personal renunciant to rescue her soul. I was stunned, back there, on the steps of Notre Dame, confounded. I wasn't judgmental, probably because my aunt was the one who told me in that solemn tone of voice she reserved for when she needed to appear solemn. Mària and I hated that tone. Instead of being judgmental, I felt a kind of envy that I couldn't explain and spent a lifetime trying to understand. Envy! Envy toward an independent-minded woman, perhaps "oppressed so hard she couldn't stand," who came to a fork in the road and had to decide whether life was worth living or not. How long did she stand at that crossroads? Did she have to wait long? Perhaps she was praying for the terror caused by fear of the noose to lift from her? No matter how long she stood at the crossroads, no matter how terrifying the noose was, her answer was no; life was not worth living. It's more likely that someone will die by jumping than by burning to death inside of a building.

Conscience and fear are appendages of the old, and I've wished since I was twenty that I could observe the world with a bit of the mind of an old woman, an old woman like the one I am now, writing these notes, supported by Jerome's pillows; debating what to tell in light of what Ms Hulme' *Nun's Story* has already revealed and what Mària and I can live with. I was too pessimistic back then; too new to the sisterhood, when Suicide, the three-syllable drumbeat began to bully an answer out of me.

Fortunately, I was dutiful to my new calling and that's what stood up to the drumbeat in my head like an Angel of the Lord and saved me from my rebellious and too pessimistic nature. Grinding my teeth became as much a part of me as my wimple. The result is that I answered as my aunt did, Beethoven's *Missa Solemnis* resonating in harmony with the drumming in my head. "Inquiring whether life is or is not worth living is a profession of doubt that defies the Commandment – an act of insubordination to Authority, a great sin." And I never mentioned my mother's suicide to Mària; I was afraid she'd think that my mother was mad. She had said often enough that I was, when finding me craving for something more generous than a kiss.

That fear was reinforced and became embedded in my mind a couple of years later in Leopoldville, where the Brussels diocese had assigned us. A dysentery patient of ours, a French economist, committed suicide. After that, I couldn't help thinking that my mother had been under the influence of a fatal mental illness as well. It's when I moved to Maison St. Jean that I concluded that my mother had committed no sin, but by then I think it was a self-serving conclusion granted because I hope for an absolution for my own end of life.

Chapter 2

Suicide, whether it be salvation or damnation, never relents. Not only that, but suicide is the con artist who cheats the Trinity out of its duty.

On September 24, 1946, another Sunday, it caught up with my uncle at the end of his driveway. Perhaps what he told me on the road back to Tournai from Forest-sur-Marque about my mother, "Being is unbearable if it's all your life has," was what he suffered from also. And, because he, too, refused to live by the axiom that suffering is preferable to death, whether the sun rose tomorrow or not, he committed suicide. I tell myself that he too got to a juncture, where he said, "I should do something about my doubt, seeing that I distrust living."

Having lived in his house twelve years, I conjectured from what I knew of him, that he wanted my aunt or a neighbor to find his body. That's why he didn't go to the Ardennes, the largest deciduous forest in Europe, the place of choice for most suicides during and even after the war. There had been so many battles fought there that unless a body is found immediately, identifying the bones searchers stumbled upon was forensically impossible.

I was certain of one thing: my uncle shot himself at the end of the driveway rather than in his room or basement because he was afraid of offending my aunt's neatness obsession by leaving anything out of place. Still, he asked me to pray for him in a note he put in his shirt pocket to make sure it would be found. "My niece is a nun." The note that was sent to me in Wembo-Nyama said, "Ask her to pray for me, too."

That note continues to fascinate me as my life passes in front of my eyes. I immediately informed Mària at the Kolwezi Orphanage for African Boys in Southern Congo that my uncle, whom she had met on the few occasions she had visited the house in Tournai, had committed suicide. She liked him because I told her he said she had a figure made for mortal sin, and he wasn't like my aunt, who insisted on treating us like children, or the poor chimney sweep who had fallen sick in her living room the previous winter and made a mess.

I collect aphorisms and stories about the God who plays jokes on humankind. My favorite is the one that says, "God promised that only good people would be found in all corners of the world. Then he made the earth round . . . and laughed."

My uncle had been a gynecologist, professionally as secure as such medical specialists could be then, what with the post-war baby boom that hit Belgium upon the end of the war in 1945. But he didn't like work. There was something about hospitals and clinics that unsettled him, made him fearful. I would often see him go hide in the basement to avoid calls for his service. His passion was hunting big games. His mood would brighten, as if sunshine was forecasted for the next six months, when his Paris hunting agent called to propose a lion or an elephant to shoot in Central or South Africa. He spent a fortune on those trips; in addition, he paid the master taxidermist in Brussels to make hunting trophies out of the dead animals he brought back from Africa. He had a game room built in the back of the villa to display them. Each new addition called for a dinner party in that room to entertain his colleagues with detailed reenactments of his exploit. Eventually his love of shooting caused him permanent hearing loss, and he needed hearing aids, which he seldom used.

Did he see himself as a wounded lion that had only a diminished existence left in his life? A farfetched conjecture, given that the constant rain in Tournai couldn't have turned the driveway into a dry African savannah.

He used what he loved the most to kill himself. Two years later, on May 12, 1948, it wasn't with a firearm but with a noose that Mària, my Mària, defied the Commandment. With her downfall, suicide inflicted its ultimate joke on me. The love of my life hung by the perfect neck that I had kissed so often from a pot's hook in her neighbor's ndako, hut, leaving her instructions nailed to the door, "Don't come in; I've killed myself." She was twenty-six years old. I was told that, when the note was discovered, the word spread with the speed of a national disaster; and as though a thief had been through the village of Nsanda seventy-eight kilometers south of Leopoldville, where she lived, to sneak off with her life, everyone jumping like goats; shouting in unison to frighten the thief away. It was getting dark when they quieted down, and they all gathered to stare at the door of the kitchen as if at the entrance to Hades – no one would go home, but no one would go in the hut to challenge the spirit that had caused the suicide of *Mama Malamu*, Good Mother, as Mària was called.

I think it was fear of the shadows on the door when banana leaves moved in the wind. That was a sign the malefic force that had caused Mària's death was still lurking about. The Congolese have a strong belief in the occurrence of murder through supernatural means. They readily accept the notion that no one's death is ever a result of natural causes, much like how hippos naturally take to water. Death means that somebody had a "tooth" against the deceased. Perhaps a spurned lover or someone filled with resentment or envy had sought revenge on Mària's life.

Ultimately, Doctor Lucien Chardant heard the news, and, acting as the Belgian colonial authorities' coroner, arrived from Leopoldville four hours later. He was the one who cut Mària down. The piece of rope made of interwoven sisal that I had found on the ship that ferried us to the Congo from Antwerp back in 1945 was what she used for a noose. I gave it to her the day of our arrival in Leopoldville as a token of our entwined lives. "I'll carry it always," she had said simply in thanks.

In her suicide note, Mària didn't mention the sisal rope. But I know it to have been her ultimate message to me. Like my uncle, she used what she prized the most to end her life. Fifty-two years have not dimmed my conclusion.

Incredibly, she was still alive when Dr. Chardant opened the kitchen door; but not surprisingly, he couldn't revive her. He was a hack who could practice no place else but the Congo.

Father Brabant, who had followed Bishop Six as Bishop of Leopoldville came in person to the Wembo-Nyama hospital to tell me of Mària's suicide. He had his accompanying priest go to my house and fetch Jerome before he told me. He then rounded up all the nurses, and, expecting me to lose my mind, they all surrounded me at the nurses' station for support.

He knew Mària to be my everything. He was the only person who ever observed us compromised – one rainy afternoon at a bus-stop overhang in Tournai, and he had named our union the "Poignant experiment." Back in Tournai, I would have lost my mind. In Wembo-Nyama, I even remained outwardly calm and have often asked myself how that was possible? The only credible explanation is that after three years in the Congo, Bantu fatalism and the belief that malefic forces surrounded us all had eaten away the little bit of optimism left in my nature, devouring it thoroughly. Progress was no longer inevitable, and we didn't learn from our mistakes. Fatalism had rubbed off on me good, and I frequently caught myself committing the sin of resignation; overwhelmed by what I witnessed happen around me.

She was the oxygen to my breath for as long as she lived. What Father Brabant and the nurses observed was my consciousness entering a protective mode and experiencing a slew of contradictory sensations. I wasn't even as shaken as I had been when my aunt told me about my mother's suicide. God forgive me, I was even glad to be rid of an obsession that had failed me. Those kind of mad sensations are what I experienced; and calmly, I told Father Brabant and the nurses that I would grieve in private in our chapel downstairs. Upon entering the chapel, I stopped breathing. The feeling of suffocating lasts a lifetime, like the sorrow of departed love. An hour later, Father Brabant interrupted my acts of contrition to the Virgin Mother, to ask me to go back with him to take care of Mària's remains. I was the only one, he said, who should have the privilege. "That's right, privilege," he stressed.

Hours following her death it began to rain over Nsanda. It hadn't rained there in so long that people had almost forgotten how it felt. Conviction being what it is, the people agreed that *Mama Malamu* had brought them rain. No less than a white nun had acknowledged the truth of Prophet Kimbangu: She had converted and died for her new faith, the Church of Jesus Christ on Earth by His special envoy Simon Kimbangu. Pilgrims came to venerate her and her prophet. They came from all over. (God forgive me for being amused by this.) A steady influx of people and cattle arrived for the rain – and to pray. Nsanda was one of the most prosperous districts in that rich, poor land when I left the Congo.

Chapter 3

I constantly regretted not considering anything that would have interfered with my love for Mària. I constantly regretted following Mària to the Congo in the quest to serve *the least of these*, the motto of the Perpetual Cross renunciants. Friends rarely end up in the same place unless love and sex are involved.

I pleaded with her that after wars like the last two inflicted on Belgium, our country was the one in need of our services. There was enough misery at home that *the least of these* were presently at the doorsteps of our convent in Liege, and I made the mistake of ironizing that Liege was far from Africa. That got me a stinging slap across the face, and a lofty reminder in that distinctive voice that could become frigidly authoritative that I had not gone to the damn Carmelites, where the gospel of meditative prayer was the vow. I had gone to the Perpetual Cross, and the Congo was the place to fulfill the order's vow to the gospel of service to *the least of these*.

"I didn't go to the Carmelites because I wasn't able to imagine life apart from you," I told her as she laid on the floor after I had hit her back as hard as I could on the shoulder; not on the beautiful face. "But I told you I didn't want to go slogging through Africa; the stories out of that Congo Free State terrify me. We are going to be absorbed into their brutality and become part of what's practiced over there."

Adamant, she wouldn't hear my plea. And that was that. She would go without me, she said; she didn't love me as I loved her. She would miss me, of course, but not being into me the way I was into her, she would manage whereas I wouldn't.

I compare myself to a rough-winged swallow lost from its flock on the way to Tournai for the summer. In time, Mària experienced the same feeling of loss.

It didn't take long for us to realize that our assumption of being exempt from the African colonization narrative was misguided. We had naively believed that we were somehow immune to the foulness, as if we were heavenly gifts from the Trinity or hailed from a utopian society rather than Europe.

Hubris or naiveté doomed us. "Ask and you shall receive," she would intone playfully a few days after our arrival in the Congo. She took steps to remedy the offense and went native; I didn't, of course.

Because Mària was a renunciant – she had left the sisterhood, but the diocese never validated her resignation. Bishop Brabant, who had been in love with her ever since we were girls in Tournai and wanted us to become Perpetual Cross sisters so we would go to the Congo, ordered that I look into the manner of her death, her funeral and burial in consecrated ground. He refused to recognize her suicide, even though her note was nailed to that kitchen door for everyone to see, as he had refused to recognize that she had joined a native sect or was having sex every day with Africans or had a child.

Mària and I had been in each other's lives since the fourth grade, when she transferred from Rumes, a suburb of Tournai, to Ecole libre Saint Michel on Rue Saint-Eleuthère where I had been since junior kindergarten.

Tournai is the oldest city in Belgium. It's in the province of Hainaut in Wallonia, ninety-four kilometers south of Brussels and twenty-seven kilometers north of the French border. Lightning had a date with thunder that morning and I cracked for her, literally split in two; and she became both the light and resonance of my life. The day is unforgettable also for having been an oddly warm and dry 1934-spring morning – nine days before my mother's death.

Wearing a white dress with a green ribbon around the waist and in her auburn long hair to go with her eyes, Mària, tall and thin, arrived unaccompanied in Miss. Gérard's class. Her distinctive face that would shortly be described as Garboesque was coldly refined.

Imagine someone under the influence of an enchantment and you've me when I saw Mària that day in 1934.

She just walks in, by herself, not inhibited at all, as new students always are and introduces herself to our teacher, Miss. Gérard. Then, standing in front of Miss Gérard's desk that's on a dais, she curtsies to the class and without Miss Gérard asking her to, she introduces herself to the class, first in French, *"Je m'appelle Mària, Mària Labienvenue. Je viens de Rumes et habite maintenant 7 Rue de Eglise Notre Dame de la Tombe. Je vais être religieuse. Je suis heureuse d'être parmi vous."* She pauses for a moment as if to give us time to absorb a voice that has importance for a pedigree; then, provocatively worldly, repeats in native-accented Dutch Flemish what she has said. Tournai is a French stronghold, and we look at one another with questioning faces. Is this Mària Labienvenue, notwithstanding her hearty French name, a Dutch gatecrasher? What eases our concern is her announcement that she intends to become a nun when she grows up. A nun, that's harmless; and we forgive her the Dutch speech. That and her saying she is happy to be among us.

Miss Gerard asks her the school's pro forma question to all new students, "What's your preferred book?"

"*Geschichte der Leben-Jesu-Forschung, The Quest of the Historical Jesus* by Albert Schweitzer[1]," she answers enthusiastically.

I'm stunned by surprise; *The Quest* happens to be my favorite book too.

Nevertheless, thereafter, classmates give her many names; all of them starting with Sis or Sister depending where on the foe to friend spectrum they are.

Anyway, I discover that nun or not she isn't a gatecrasher at all but an upper-middle class mutineer, who will let no opportunity pass to thwart whatever she considers "bourgeois" narrow-mindedness.

"I have a responsibility to that belief and never let myself forget it," she tells me years later as earnestly as if she were staking her life on this so-called belief. "If you have the means, you have the power to bring joy into your life; do what makes you happy!"

In hindsight, Mària was perhaps a mutant; certainly a hippie. In the '60's she would've been called a Flower Child. How she got that way, I wish I knew because I wanted desperately to know everything about her; be in her soul, to be acquainted with the vital force that drove her, her essence and inner Màriaesque energy.

People are naturally sympathetic toward the underdog and the needy, especially the helpless. I suspect that Mària was

---

1.   http://en.wikipedia.org/wiki/Albert_Schweitzer

endowed with that quality but to a misshapen degree, predisposing her toward those she saw as disadvantaged, *the least of these*. And she gave in to that particular inclination as reflexively as metals give in to magnets. I met a woman who upon the onset of menopause became fixated on saving strayed dogs and cats to such an extent that her life was swallowed into her mania. People are saddled with proclivities over which they have little say, and as they meander through their time on earth, like Mària, they are prisoners of their individual castles that no maid service can tidy-up.

I look back through sixty-six years to that day and affirm that back then you knew five minutes after meeting Mària that she had some kind of innate attraction to the disadvantaged as if programmed to champion societies' wretched. I'd say do-gooder, but the term has a naive connotation that doesn't fit Mària, who was more self-centered or knew more about what she was about and was more purposeful in the sense of calculated than anyone I'd ever known when it came to what she wanted. An angel was beside her, ringing the bell that reminded her of who she was and what she stood for.

However, in novels I've read, the character that comes closest to being like her is Melanie Hamilton.

The label of socialist would later be affixed to Mària, and her ambition in life was to join a convent. By the time she turned fourteen, socialist and renunciant were already her flags.

When it comes to describing her, you'd have to mention her auburn colored hair, Garboesque features, and luminous green eyes. She also has a gorgeous figure and happens to be a teenager with strong socialist views. Interestingly, she believes that becoming a nun is the path to fulfilling her inner drive. No other depiction would do justice to her innate equilibrium. She was never labeled a communist most likely because of her desire to become a nun.

When I think of her personality, I can't help but be reminded of Icarus, the tragic hero who dared to defy the natural order of things by flying too close to the sun with wings made of wax. His story serves as a cautionary tale, allowing the Greeks to attribute his downfall to fate and invent tragedy.

The Greeks were on to something, though; for what is fate, if not one's nature unfolding, indifferent, and blind. We live not as we wish but as our nature lets us. "The fault, dear Brutus, is in our nature," Miss Louise, our ninth grade world literature teacher would singsong maniacally.

The tragic hero, in a quest to gain control over his life, tries to make logical decisions, unaware of the all-encompassing influence of illusion. The absurd is what comes from thinking he has the means to turn off nature and get into the cockpit of his life. I couldn't help but roll my eyes at Miss Louise's decision to treat me like a leaf in the wind. That's because at that time, myself and the majority of my classmates were completely captivated by the exciting idea of being destined to have endless possibilities, doomed to have options. Through the passage of time, I have come to realize, though it has been a difficult lesson, that the idea of choice is often just another illusion, there to keep us out of insane asylums.

I used to think every time I read something about hippies or about California that Mària, no matter what, would've been at home in San Francisco in the sixties, a flower child in sync with her nature and fate. I wish I had seen California; maybe it would've told me a bit about Mària, who called herself a *de zwerver,* nomadic bird, a name she borrowed from the '30's German youth movement that opposed the authoritarian culture of big cities in favor of nature and life of the spirit. Sister de Zwerver, she said she was.

The tragedy of Mària is that she didn't follow her nature: instead of going to San Francisco, she went to the Congo. Mothers should warn their children that the captain and guide of life is indifferent to their wishes. Mària thought that by following the Eternal Light she would see her way through the darkness of indifference. She failed because she went to the Congo instead of San Francisco.

In preparing her for the new school, her mother told her about Tournai's prejudice against the Dutch Flemish. To Mària, prejudice is "petit bourgeois," her archenemy. "Because petit bourgeois are loath to accept their inferior position in society, they search for others to place beneath them," she told me.

Following her mother's briefing, she asked one of the family maids who was from Dutch Ghent to help her learn her introduction by heart just so that she could affront us with her saying it as if she were Dutch herself. Come what may, she remained oblivious to what Ecole libre Saint Michel thinks of her, or she sticks her tongue out at her adversaries or curses them like an Ostend longshoreman.

It takes her two weeks to take up the school's dress code, white blouse, blue skirt, blue blazer and black shoes. She is nothing if not upper-middle class herself, with the accent on snob, if you had asked me then. Still, that spring morning, I couldn't wait to copy her. In time, I'll want nothing more than be a footnote to her life. My impressionistic heart has found its hero and muse and would not let go. By the time we take our baccalaureate from Saint Michel, I even write like her.

Before she walked in, we were reading Victor Hugo's *Les Misérables.* Miss Gérard must have been as taken with her voice as we were, for as soon as Mària completed telling us the title of her favorite book, Miss Gérard asked her to read the scene by the river where Inspector Javert catches up with Jean Valjean and ends up in the Seine.

Four days after my mother's funeral, my aunt came to Saint Michel to tell the administration that she had taken me in as a foster child. My father has moved to Lille, and it's clear he doesn't want me to go with him. I am an only child. My mother's sister and her husband, who live in Tournai, are the only other people in my family. After much persuasion from my uncle, my aunt has finally agreed to take care of me as her ward.

I remember the day well; the sky was not as overcast as usual and you could tell by the warmth in the air that there was a chance we would have a real summer with real sunshine, the kind you feel on your face that burns you. Back in 1934, rain was a curse for most people, but rain comforted me like a blanket on a chilly night. I have just read a biography of the celebrated American humorist and, like me, an alcoholic, W. C Fields, who relished the sound of falling rain so much that on his deathbed, his friends put a water hose on the roof of his bungalow so he could hear the sound. I've sent a note to the administrator of Maison Tournai that if it's not raining on my day, on pain of Maison Tournai being left out of my will, he should see to it that what was done for W.C. Fields is done for me. Because our weather was so dreary in 1934, we measured events by whether the sun shone, for how long, and how warm it was. Droughts and forest fires are now cursing us a thousand times over; in a short time, the Ardennes Forest will be devoid of vegetation because the rains have moved elsewhere.

I was too young to understand what it would mean to have to live under my aunt's roof. However, when in the cafeteria at lunch seated by ourselves, Mària, who was the most honestly sympathetic toward me when Miss Gerard told the class of my loss, put my head on her shoulder to console me.

I know what it means to hear her say she loves me. I saw that she knew what it implied and would learn later what being willing to be seduced also meant. Removed from prying eyes, I kissed her deeply in gratitude, and she put her hand under my panties to touch me there. I think it was then that I dedicated my life to her. But it could've been another instance; there were so many. What's for sure is that natural selection has nothing over whom one loves or one's sexual preference.

The first-time Mària and I went to Notre Dame de Tournai with the express intention of speaking to the parish priest about convents was a Thursday in late spring 1938. We were sixteen. Thursdays were a school's half day then and around midday we would drift with our classmates to the bus stop to catch the number 5 to downtown where we would hang all afternoon around the coffee shops, bookstores, nickelodeon. I don't know whether Mària planned the visit. She told me no, but she was an enigmatic girl, and I wasn't sure.

We were in a rush to catch the bus on Thursday because we were running late due to a German test. Unfortunately, we didn't have time to store our blue and white school uniforms in a school locker with the rest of our belongings. The rain had stopped; the rough-winged swallows, a well-known sight in Tournai, had already made their way back from Africa and were darting around in a frenzy, looking for their nests. One of them left a surprise on Mària's right sleeve.

I saw it but she didn't, and I thought it wise not to tell her. Urban birds were all dirty pigeons as far as she was concerned. (Her first year in Tournai, she wrote the mayor to ask him to forbid the feeding of pigeons in Tournai, writing that the pigeons would thus spend more time looking for food and less time reproducing. The mayor invited her to his office. "I'll go if you go with me," she proposed. Her mother wanted to go too; and Mària, not yet up to refusing her, reluctantly agreed. The mayor received us promptly at the appointed time and while we were sipping his Lipton Tea he offered Mària an after-school job going around parks explaining to the people of Tournais why they shouldn't feed the pigeons. Mària was thrilled, but her parents didn't care for the idea, and nothing ever came of it.) I, on the other hand, had no problems with urban birds, especially the singing ones; they fascinated me.

That Thursday, the number 5 was fuller than usual of students going like us to the town center; exuberant, the school bus is a recess on wheels. Summer break was starting in a few weeks, and we were all excited about "*la belle*," our name for summer vacation, the beloved time of the year. Only a few hadn't changed out of the school uniform, and we stood out.

Around the corner of Avenue Chaussade de Douai, the cathedral steeples came into view and Mària, who was as excited by the approaching vacation as everyone else on the bus, suddenly bent to my ear to whisper a challenge about convents. "*Chiche*", she interjected, "I dare you." I recovered quickly from my surprise and even had time to make accepting cheerful. She gave me a long inquiring look, not convinced I was sincere, as I wasn't sure whether she had planned the visit to the cathedral all along.

When the bus reached the cathedral stop, it was raining again. I opened my umbrella, and, wanting to show her how keen I was, I jumped out first, and laughing, we raced to the door of the diocese attached to the cathedral's north side, our opened umbrellas pitching left and right with each of our strides. Mària wasn't wearing her sport bra, and her large breasts slowed her down. I was first at the diocese's door. We entered a poorly lit foyer that had only a high-ceilinged yellow stained-glass window to supply light. Directly under it, a tonsured monk was sitting at a low desk, filling missals from a box full of prayer cards at his feet. His large black eyes registered delight that we had interrupted his drudgery, or else he couldn't believe his ears that we had come because we were interested in convents and wanted to talk to the parish priest. "Father Brabant will love you," he said excitedly in Mària's direction, as he picked up the phone to call the parish priest.

Father Brabant, who would be so consequential to our story, was a Walloon priest from the town of Waterloo, in the province of Walloon Brabant, serving, when we first met him, the French community of Tournai. In his forties, he was of medium height, ascetically thin, and pleasant looking, with gray hair surrounding a baldpate and a somber, compassionate face that had no creases from laughter or smiles. Strength of character didn't show in his tiny nose and weak chin but in his powerful intense blue eyes.

As though ours was a celestial visitation, he remained standing looking at us opened mouth for quite a while. When recovered and able to pry his eyes from Mària, he left us in his office to go look for one of the diocese nuns. He came back fifteen minutes later accompanied by a short, ample elder renunciant with facial hair, including a visible mustache, whom he introduced as Reverend Mother Bertrande from the Perpetual Cross order. Her eyes, magnified by thick glasses, picked out Mària, the moment she entered the office.

Father Brabant must have said something to her about Mària's sleeve, for she has come with a washcloth. He points to the spot, and she bends to it. Puzzled Mària looks at me. I make a face that it's nothing. Father Brabant then decides that he will do the cleaning. It's more indispensable that Mother Bertrande talk to us. She gives him the washcloth a little reluctantly it seems and ambles to the back of the room to get a chair that she places in front of us; then she and I watch Father Brabant wipe the bird's poop off Mària's sleeve. He keeps his hand on Mària's arm longer than necessary, but perhaps I am imagining things. All the same, he does a commendable job cleaning her sleeve.

Like Mària, Mother Bertrande has a melodious deep voice. The sort you inquire about and eagerly listen to. The sort you love in a sermon. She gives us a virtual tour of her order, its history, its rules, and its service. When she pauses, it's to get us out of Father Brabant's office, by inviting us to her own place for tea. He is reluctant to give us up, especially Mària, I'm sure; and he's getting up to go with us, but Mother Bertrande must have made a gesture for he sits back down behind his desk and asks us to come afterward to his office before we leave the diocese.

We follow Mother Bertrande down a long dark hallway covered on both sides with pictures of priests to an office smaller but more cheerful than Father Brabant's, her reception area, she calls it. Brightly illuminated, it gives out the sense that a woman lives there. Bookcases, as if to shield the four walls, are all around, except on the part of the wall, where a crucifix hangs behind a large desk. Surprisingly avant-garde in design, the crucifix is unlike any Mària and I have ever seen. A nephew has made it for her with wrought iron at a school's shop, she tells us, when she sees us examining it. In the years since, most crucifixes have shed their classical design and become like the one we saw in Mother Bertrande's office in 1938. Forty years later, that cross will find its way to the Vatican and on top of John Paul II's pastoral staff.

Included in the tour of the office she gives us are various dolls from all over the world, sitting on top of the bookcases like little people engaged in telling fairy-tales to whomever walks in. Sisters from her order send her the dolls from countries where they work, knowing that she is an avid collector. While she is making us tea, we look at her books. Except for a few on Jansenism and about church fathers the bookshelves contain mostly new volumes by and about German philosophers including Marx. We look at one another in surprise. She sees that her books have thrown us a *verwondering*, a wonder, as we say in Belgium, and she chuckles. "Like most people who look at my library," she says, "you expected to see only missals, catechisms and magnificats, right?" Mària answers in the affirmative by nodding, and I do the same. "We're devoted readers," Mother Bertrande explains, talking to us as if we were novices. "And we read all kinds of books all the time. Today, we read about the coming war and what it will mean to our poor congregants. Dislocation farther than the eye can see and the mind can understand is what. As historical players, we have an obligation to maintain the church's ecosystem against ideologies opposed to the Good News. Questions about everything are disrupting our world and confusing in unimaginable ways the people we serve. The utopia of Marxism is the most alluring now, and the intelligentsia in the Third World is having a grand ball with it; but thank God they haven't the brains to be socialists yet. To compete, we're forced to become experts in these ideologies. Compared to Marxism, witchcraft is a fairy tale. In Africa, it's both Marxism and the race consciousness philosophy called Negritude we contend with. And there are Bantu churches more or less related to Christianity springing up all the time. We read these books that you see here so that we can address the concerns of our people."

Mària exclaims, "We have read a bit about Marxism but didn't appreciate it because it denies the Trinity's existence." When I hear her say that, I lower my head at once so that Mother Bertrande doesn't see the shock I know is on my face. Mària can fib with such aplomb that she always takes me off guard.

Remembering our school days now, I don't think there was a sixteen-year old anywhere who was more fascinated by or knew more about Marxism than Mària. "It will upend humanity and release the brotherhood of man on the world to reflect Christ's providence. It will shepherd in the fraternal age He promised," she told my uncle who was a member of the POB, the Belgian Workers Party, once, when she was visiting me. He didn't know what Mària was talking about and later told me, "Your friend, the one who wants to be a nun, is *machtige eigenaardige,*" nuts. She was just ahead of her time, a 1938 Liberation Theology promoter and behavioral scientist, who thought socialism to be synonymous with brotherhood and being virtuous in the world. But at sixteen, she knew well enough to hide and go around such convictions. In the end, she would give in to her anger and stubbornness because she was tired of waiting. Then, she would try to go beyond Rules and attitudes. And fall.

In 1938, Mària was just as interested in Marxism as she was in convents. She thought that her interest in socialism went well with her calling to become a nun. I didn't know why she told Mother Bertrande she didn't like Marxism at the time. "I wanted that old butch to think I was a blank slate so she wouldn't have any ideas about me already," she told me on the way home when I asked her about lying. Mària was more experienced and wise than I was. She was also faster on her feet.

Chapter 4

In Mother Bertrande's office, we sit around a small table next to the window and watch the rain; and Mother Bertrande serves us tea she says is from the colony of Ruanda-Urundi in Central Africa. The rain is surly and makes us reflective. Someone observing us would conclude that we were praying to the rain's creator, thankful for its wonder. The rain is one of my sanctuaries; I feel secure when it falls.

After a couple of sips of her tea, Mother Bertrande asks us to tell her about ourselves. It's raining, so I feel safe enough to go first. But what is there to tell? I start with a chronological account of my life – I was born in Tournai on March 7, 1922 and so on and add more details as I go along. Mother Bertrande interrupts me only at the part where I lose my mother to tell me that she's sorry and will pray for my mother's soul. She sounds sincere, and I thank her. Mària smiles. And I wish she hadn't because she's now given Mother Bertrande the impression that she likes her. It's her turn, and as far as her physical life is concerned, like me, she only tells our hostess what we have figured out she expects to hear. We're both pious and pure. Like me, Mària has had a normal childhood. Like me she has friends, goes to school and church. Mària's desire to become a renunciant is the only thing that makes us different.

Mària then suddenly switches tactic, off with the material and on with the emotional and the spiritual part of what she wants Mother Bertrande to hear. No more platitudes; it's time to make the most of today's visit to the diocese; show genuine interest. Mother Bertrande hears that a life of church service is what Mària is interested in. She nods in acknowledgment of Mària's profession of faith and service and keenness to sacrifice. Mària has been studying this for a long time; she knows what tenor to give sacrifice. Sacrifice, the magic word that turns tigers into kittens. She picks up the tempo of her narrative, and I watch her face radiate sincerity; then I watch her sincerity mesmerize Mother Bertrande to the point of experiencing bliss. Mària, worldly, is always an irresistible Mària.

So effective is Mària that when she stops talking, Mother Bertrande's beaming face and moist eyes convey the conviction that Mària, and by extension the girl who has come with her, should be on the fast track to sisterhood, renunciants of the Perpetual Cross order. Mother Bertrande's pastel-colored face has turned pink; she looks twenty years younger, through the excitement she has allowed herself to experience. It will be her privilege, she stammers, to be our novice mentor and work with us on our letter of intent to the Mother Superior. Then she pleads with us to consider no order other than The Perpetual Cross's, assuring us that Mària and I wouldn't be separated because it wouldn't be beneficial to us and to the order.

"What impresses me the most about you," she says to us, as earnestly as I've no doubt she has ever allowed herself to say anything, "is that you're already aware that humanity needs your sacrifice; and since you don't want to be locked up in an ivory tower in a desert somewhere just reflecting on the woes of the world, you're going to walk these woes with your own two feet – like the Lord himself. Young women like you take the cross to nurse the sick, teach the children, administer the empire and take the light of civilization to the darkness of the poor pagans. The church carries on thanks to you."

"Has your school read *Divina Commedia*?" she asks.

"I answer, yes."

"That madman, Alighieri, is a heretic," she tells us haughtily. "Christ doesn't condemn *the least of these*, who through no fault of their own do not know Him. For Alighieri to say that Christ is unjust is a mortal sin. The mission of the Perpetual Cross order is to bring His light to *the least of these*, by serving them, not by reviling them. Our sisters are in the Congo, Ruanda-Urundi, working as teachers, nurses and administrators there. Without them Belgium has no empire; leaving us at the mercy of the European powers." Mària and I look at each other; Mother Bertrande's statement is heartfelt and passionate, but it's more than we expected. She sees the look but doesn't comment.

It's late afternoon already. Time has passed without us noticing. The rain continues to fall with the hours, and I feel suspended between a momentous 1938-day and my desire to remain at Mària's side. Mària, on the other hand, is excited by the significant step she has taken on the course to sisterhood this afternoon in the year of our lord 1938. If this had been her room, she would have had one of her maddening orgasms. Mother Bertande will remain oblivious that it's more than mere vocation with Mària, a left-wing extremist who believes that renunciant and socialist are mutually inclusive and have one face. Whenever I had doubts about continuing on this path and the anxiety became unbearable, I considered saving myself by destroying Mària's unique concept of sisterhood, by going to Mother Bertrande and telling her: Mària is a socialist, Mària is another Jezabel, or Mària will be a wolf in the fold.

Mària gives me a long look to assess what I'm thinking. Satisfied, she winks our intimate wink. Any other time, I would be pleased. However, on this particular afternoon in 1938, my love for her is dimmed by the sense that she is about to cross the Rubicon of her life here in the Tournai diocese. She's leading me along, and the sense of being suspended between a historic 1938 day and my desire to stay by her side grows stronger. It's as if I am climbing the church's steeple and my fear of heights is making me sick.

Mother Bertrande regains control over her excitement. Patient again she walks us once more through the doors we've to pass to become the young women who take the cross to nurse the sick, teach the children, administer the empire and take the light of civilization to the darkness of *the least of these.*

She looks at me every once in a while, but her eyes are always on Mària. Mària isn't a flirt; if she were, I would have gone crazy. She is actually distant, if that's the opposite of flirt. However, a look about her that some of our classmates who study Greek call *"alpha,"* makes her seem like Tinkerbelle sprinkling her fairy dust to exert a magnetic pull over everyone she meets. Like pets waiting for a bone, they want to please her, take care of her; be around her. Ever since she can remember, ordinary people have said that she has *"du chien,"* sex appeal.

People who are jealous of her and whose childishness competes with their vulgarity say that she is a coquette. One thing Mària is never is this. She is too used to being hit on and is too afraid of being raped. In fact, sometimes I wonder if her obsessive interest in convents isn't a way to put her look on ice. Also, I've noticed that Mària wants to get to the convent more quickly the more people talk about war. Remembrance of what

German soldiers inflicted on women just twenty years earlier is routine, and I wonder if she does not consider the convent a refuge. I know many girls who did.

Mother Bertrande's welcome, explanations, and support have also catalyzed Mària's heart as effectively as a Cupid arrow. I've seldom seen her so animated. Dreams are fed by what is attainable, while hopelessness is fed by what is not. Mària now has a powerful glimpse of what is possible. That glimpse has put her on a high that any opiate addict would kill for.

It is possible to become a renunciant, not impossible as she feared. She is so happy that she throws caution to the wind and brags that it was her idea to go to the diocese this afternoon to ask about the convent. She's pretty confident that when it comes to her beliefs, she won't have to make any bargains or sacrifices. She can remain unchanged. Renunciant is an outdated term that no longer signifies a complete relinquishment of all possessions and commitments. She can hold onto her beliefs about the ideal way for people to live and how society should be structured. There's no need for her to alter her true self.

Obstinately, she visualizes serving *the least of these* her way. That's why she's bursting with excitement. For the time being, she is fulfilled; Mother Bertrande's orientation has surpassed all her expectations.

There are stories of girls being forced into convents, especially in the farming areas of the north and the poor suburbs of Brussels. These girls end up in Africa. Mària, giddy with anticipation, isn't one of them, and not only because of her class. She isn't going to be recruited; she's going to demand to join.Volunteers are going to look up to her as a saint.

For a while longer, she asks the questions; I, dutifully, take notes that I'll plead we review later.

It's been over two hours, and Father Brabant must have been tired of waiting. He's come to Mother Bertrande's door, and we hear him turn the doorknob. It's locked. A look of fright comes to Mària's face. When did Mother Bertrande lock the door? We didn't see her make the gesture that kept Father Brabant out for two hours either. The two must have played this game before, for she whispers in our direction, "He will break the door with his shoulder to get at you." Strange, isn't it? On our first day in the institution Mària is dying to join, we get an indication of what must go on between fathers and sisters in this diocese.

Mària has a word of the week she practices using all day long, a seven-day nuisance. Last week the word was *soupçon*. This day in 1938, I am suspicious of the two clerics who've put Mària on the road to the convent she dreams of. If I tell my aunt that I'm guarded with a member of the clergy, she'll be shocked and order acts of contrition for an entire month, after I've washed my mouth with soap. Adults are in awe of clerics. Conversely, my generation tolerates them and takes a cruel pleasure at mocking them. We're French, and it's at the church of republican secularism that our generation prays. This is 1938. Vive la Revolution of 1789!

Father Brabant has arrived uninvited with a ready apology for disrupting Mother Bertrande's meeting with two uncommonly attractive prospects for postulancy. Other than welcoming platitudes she says nothing. But her short frowns show that she is irritated. Maybe this is an example of what she meant when she said that women in the church are treated like second-class citizens and have to carry the cross of the Lord's command to help *the least of these.* I check my notes to make sure I wrote down what she said about women in the church so I can talk about it with Mària. I tell myself, 'There's a lot to talk about,' because I know it will be hard to get Mària to talk about the sad parts of our visit to the diocese this afternoon. Her vocation is a high-minded obstacle because of how aggressive it is.

Father Brabant goes to the round table by the window and sits down. Outside, it's pouring rain — the masterpiece that everyone knows and loves. After he's done looking out the window, he looks at us. He seems uncomfortable, in a sheepish sort of way and is silent. In this small office full of books by and about German philosophers, there is a tug-of-war going on between the clerics, as there must be in all bureaucracies. The difference is that this bureaucracy usually keeps its tugging and pulling behind baroque walls, away from the always-curious eyes of congregants, who then make up rumors about what they can't see with their own eyes. Mària and I are lucky to be able to see what's going on this afternoon in 1938.

Between Mother Bertrande and Father Brabant, the tug and pull are not between equals. Mother Bertrande knows to pass us over to Father Brabant. However, like all subordinates, she has ways of going around her disadvantage. Before he arrived, she made us promise to meet with her after mass Sunday. And while he reflects on the rain once again, ingeniously, she tells us the story of Francis of Assisi. She clocks the time we told her we have to leave to go catch the bus for home with the end of the story, St. Francis's receiving his stigmata. That way, she leaves Father Brabant no time with Mària and me.

Nevertheless, Father Brabant has the last word as the story ends and St. Francis is struck with the marks of the cross. Mother Bertrande can only nod when he says that he will walk us out as we get up to leave.

In the hallway, he talks fast and walks slowly, a delaying tactic that can't work today because it's late afternoon and we've to get our things before five o'clock from the school's locker or the principal will *consign* us, the term for having to come to the school on a Sunday as punishment. We walk faster; consequently, he puts his arm around my shoulders to slow us down, pissing Mària off. She sprints to the foyer, and I follow her, leaving Father Brabant to nurse his embarrassment in the hallway. Mària gets to the foyer's door first. The tonsured monk is still at his little desk filling missals with prayer cards under the stained-glass window that the rain has turned to a grayish-orange color.

"Thank you." We shout as we fly by him; and he raises his head numbly to watch us run by and bang the door open to get out as if bulls are after us. We left our umbrellas in Mother Bertrande's umbrella stand and this time we've to run faster to the bus stop to get out of the downpour. But like the teenagers we sometimes are, we laugh as we splash our way to the overhang. Mària gets to the bus stop first, only because I love feeling the rain falling on me, and I hang back to enjoy it. When I catch up with her inside the bus stop's overhang, she reaches out for me, and I spin against the glass, her mouth over mine. Maria had that look, but I have no time to react to what I knew was coming. When lust was on her, she was out of her wits. Her beautiful mouth would stretch disproportionally in a clown's smile/ an ugly rictus. Then her eyes would become slits/ filmed over, as if having become sightless, and her skin would dew over like dew grass in the morning. Finally, frissons would rack her as if a spirit has gotten hold of her and she is fighting to be let go.

She plants her tongue in my mouth, sucking the breath out of me; and she fights me to lift my skirt so she can put her finger in me. When she screams, she sounds like an angel who has been taken to heaven through the alchemy of lust. Has anyone seen us through the downpour? Thank God for the rain. One more reason to love it. I look around to make sure. Someone in a black cassock is standing as still as a statue under an oversized umbrella on the steps of the parvis across the road. He's staring at us through the glass. Mària has seen him too. It's a figure whose face we can't make out through the rain. Deflated, she's speechless. I try to think and blurt out the first explanation that comes to mind,

"We were so happy with our visit to the diocese that we couldn't resist hugging each other in the overhang, as soon as we got out of the rain. If someone asks, that's what we'll say. Anyway, he couldn't tell you were trying to ravish me through this downpour."

All she can think of saying is, "I've to stop screaming like that." It's her way of trying to prevent a fight between us, for I've told her over and over again to stop with the screams, and she has told me a thousand times to stop with wine tasting.

Having scored an A+ with the two diocese's clerics and with herself, Mària has awakened to find her dream of a convent as prelude to her future.

I don't recall her exuding passion the first time she mentioned wanting to be a nun in 1934, back in fourth grade, when she introduced herself to the class, poised and worldly. It was just the statement of a fact. Stereotyping being ignorance's favorite surrogate, I probably told myself, nuns don't look like that girl. Who will take seriously that such a beauty wants to be a nun? Raised on Stendhal's *The Red and the Black,* I learned that impoverished men join the army, criminal gangs, the police, or the seminary to bypass their social condition; women enter convents for the same reason. Mària was as far from being poor as the North Pole is from the South Pole. But she wanted to become a nun just as much as the characters in Stendhal's masterpiece.

When I first met Mària, we talked about her ambition. I felt disconnected because I couldn't relate to her goal; she, on the other hand, acted as if it were the most natural thing in the world. Not until we were heavily into each other did I realize that this idea had grown with her and filled a space in her life like air in a bubble. This decision to join a convent was so ingrained that Mària and her decision were two sides of the same coin. She was more grown up than I was. She made decisions and always did her best to stick to them.

Before that afternoon in 1938 at the Tournai diocese, I didn't think this whole thing about convents would lead anywhere. From my point of view, Mària was chasing after something she couldn't catch. This was a fixation she had to deal with until she grew up. At some point, her little girls' dream would run into the steel wall of reality and other hopes.

Mària was nervous that the church's establishment would reject her because she didn't look the part. Even my uncle, no lecher, observed that she had a figure built for sin, a superficial observation, to be sure, but a telling anecdote against the fulfillment of her dream. Her fear grew as she grew into a voluptuously beautiful woman. The church might find it difficult to accept her.

She was not a model for a nun, who was expected to be plain if not androgynous. Having striking looks was considered offensive, guaranteeing she wouldn't be admitted. But how do you reconcile with God who made you eye-catching? She argued that I looked the part, if only because I wasn't as striking as she was. Surprisingly, we were both the same size and wore each other's clothes. But it's true that I tended toward the androgynous. "This infernal thing," as she called *avoir du chien,* sex appeal, obsessed her, and she spoke constantly about having the right pedigree in mind but not in body.

On the streets, she accosted renunciants of all orders to question them. Mostly, they answered in platitudes, probably in recognition that she was *machtige eigenaardige,* nuts. And she read about convents with a dedication that bordered on medieval. She found corroborative evidence for her apprehension in the precept that a nun cannot bring attention to herself, and cannot be a source of desire for the devil to inflict his temptations on the poor in spirit. Her auburn hair, for example, would be considered an adornment. She had it cut *a la garconne,* a short boyish haircut. The result was disastrous, for the new haircut emphasized her Garboesque shaped face, making her even more striking. She had her first cigarette on the day of that haircut.

Chapter 5

It came as a shock to her that Mother Bertrande and Father Brabant would fawn over her as much as they did, lifting the trepidation that the church would consider her application a scam. She concurred eagerly with Mother Bertrande that the spur of the moment's visit to the diocese was a sign.

Suddenly, formal vows don't seem impossible anymore or even that distant in the future. Suddenly, excitement replaces gloom, and Mària is as horny as a rabbit. Suddenly, she's looking forward to an instructive novitiate period. Suddenly, I don't know where Mària's departure will leave me.

As we get on the bus back to Saint Michel, I hear her mutter, "It's unnatural," under her breath. I can't ask her what is because it's late afternoon; the bus is crowded, and we've no room to talk.

In the bus, I'm myself experiencing a strange sensation it takes me a while to identify as conceit: Oh my God, I tell myself, I'm feeling superior to the other passengers for having been to the diocese to talk to the clerics about Mària entering a convent. It's a sickening feeling, but I have no control over it, and I imagine not quite in jest that I'm a hostage; experiencing a manipulation of the devil.

Mària had taken the same feeling to a higher level and called it "unnatural."

When we get off, I ask her about it. "It's just a smug feeling of superiority that came over me, and I couldn't believe it," she answers, dejectedly, as she rushes inside Saint Michel with me following to retrieve our school bags. That's all she says about it because she is preoccupied. She isn't communicating. Then abruptly she turns to me and announces that we should walk to Rue de Eglise Notre Dame de la Tombe to thrash out what Mother Bertrande and Father Brabant told us.

Mària doesn't say my house like everyone else. *My* house is the one in Rumes she left four years ago not the one on Rue de Eglise.

"Are you unhappy here," I once asked?

"No, not exactly. It's that I don't care for cities. I was also used to Rumes. I was born there, you know." That's what she says. I know she's putting me off. She gives bland answers when she doesn't want you to pry. I have adapted to her idiosyncrasies; nevertheless, we have the passionate fights only people who trust each other beyond the mundane have. The other thing about the house is that Mària doesn't say it's on Rue de Eglise like everyone else who lives on that street. She insists on the full title, Rue de Eglise Notre Dame de la Tombe, to make sure, it seems, that you have no doubt she doesn't belong there.

Fortunately, the rain has paused, and we can walk to her house eight blocks from our school. From there my uncle will pick me up at dinnertime. Having no umbrella we walk fast. A downcast Mària makes me wait for her. The rain is coming, I tell her; and she joins me only to fall back again. The exuberance experienced upon leaving the diocese is gone, and the apprehension is back, smothering her mood. She's literally stewing in it. I do all the talking while she's next to me; going over what Mother Bertrande told us.

Then, as if released from detention, her voice blurts out, "It could've been only one priest standing across the road from the bus stop like that. He was behind us. Remember?" I'd forgotten about the priest across the road while Mària was fondling me; but she hadn't and was rehashing the picture in her mind and obsessing about it. I walk back to where she is, to plead with her that we couldn't see his features, which means that from across the road, he couldn't see ours through the downpour.

She shakes her head, "He saw us, I tell you," she chokes. And I tell myself that not even Mària knows how deep her convent ambition goes.

Mària's house is a late 19th century three-story structure surrounded by other old upper-middle class homes on the northwest side of Rue de Eglise Notre Dame de la Tombe. We arrive just as the rain begins again.

During the walk, Mària and I decide that we'll go back to the diocese the following Thursday and face Father Brabant. Whatever he says he's seen, we'll deny. It was raining. That's our alibi.

Mrs. Labienvenue, Mària's mother, is a tall woman, taller than her husband, an industrialist, meaning a man of wealth, whom I've met only twice since 1934. She looks much older than her forty-one years because she wears outdated dresses and puts lots of rouge on small parts of her cheeks so that she will look like beloved Queen Astrid who died in 1935. Mària told me that she had a 'blue fear' of dentists and is afraid to show her bad teeth, and that's why she never smiles.

She comes to greet Mària not with a smile but with kisses on both cheeks. Mària doesn't kiss her back but gives her an annoyed look. That's why Mrs. Labienvenue boasts of Mària's independence of mind to teachers and neighbors and claims to be proud of her willfulness too. Mothers usually give me welcome kisses at other homes, more so after my mother died. Here, Mrs. Labienvenue tolerates me for Mària's sake and says no more than hello to me. Sometimes she remarks about my constant presence at Mària's side. "Doesn't she have other friends?" she asks pointedly when she passes Mària in the hallway.

Thinking of Mària's mother back then leads me to my own mother. She was petite, pretty and was not afraid of dentists. She kept an eye on me in a busybody underhanded sort of way that annoyed me to no end. Seldom, however, did she punish me or embarrassed me with kisses in front of friends. When I was passed on to my aunt in 1934, I entered the household of a tidiness-obsessed woman. If Mària came to meet me there, she'd never go in but sat on one of the benches in the manicured front garden sometimes talking to my uncle whom she liked because he belonged to the POB, the Belgian Workers Party, and discussed politics with her and listened to her expound on her understanding of socialism, although he seldom knew what she was talking about.

In my aunt's house, the appointment of every item reflected the compulsive mania the lady of the house suffered from. Things had to be in symmetrical order and arrayed in martial exactitude or both my uncle and I would catch the consequences, my uncle for allowing me to fall into the sin of untidiness; I, for being a messy creature of the incorrigible kind. In the end, me more than my uncle received the brunt of my aunt's fixations. I would've to come home immediately after school. Another word, Mària would be forbidden to me for a week or more as punishment. I suffered this regime for four years.

For Mària and her mother, it's a case of the mother making do with what she cannot change. Mària listens to the maid from Ghent, named "*la petite Marie*," Little Marie, with better grace than she does her mother. I never know why exactly. Maybe Little Marie is the maid who fondled her in her bath, the one she told me about. A rather intimate look comes over Little Marie's face whenever she addresses Mària, and she seems to be always hovering at Mària's door when I visit. Mària makes grousing sounds when we are in her room, and she thinks the maid is hanging around the door. The only answer she gives me when I ask about Little Marie's peculiarities is that the maid is protective of her. She once said that the maid was proprietary of her and something about Little Marie knowing her since she was a little girl. Mària has an exaggerated sense of privacy, a mania that forbids anyone, even me, access to her inner sanctum. On every anniversary of her death, I end my prayer with a mea culpa, telling myself that I'm to blame for letting her make a fetish of privacy to the point of giving in to suicide without confiding in anyone. I rationalize, of course; it's part of the ambiguity old age has imposed on me. At least it isn't sour grapes or anything like that anymore.

It's Thursday and it's raining, but we've our new umbrellas that we swear we'll not forget on the bus as we do all the time or at the diocese. We put our effects in the school's lockers; but, even if we've time today, we don't change out of our school uniforms. Mària has determined that it's better to keep the look that worked for us the week before. That look will bring us luck again.

The Number 5 is just as crowded as it was last Thursday and the anticipation is even more upbeat. Recess is in the air, and we breathe it hungrily. At the Notre Dame de Tournai stop, Mària and I get off together. It's still raining, and we open our umbrellas so automatically, we don't know we've done it; it's as routine as breakfast in the morning. Today, we don't run as we did last week; we rather use the time to rehash how we're going to comport ourselves in front of Farther Brabant. I'm not as apprehensive as Mària, who has staked her future on what the father thinks he saw.

When I think of this today, it fascinates me that not once did we give the father the benefit of the doubt that maybe he was an open-minded man with an appreciation for love in all its complexities and splendor.

The church's piazza, which starts at the bus stop and ends at the door of the diocese, is almost one-quarter kilometer long. It seems designed to give visitors plenty of walking time to ponder what they're going to say when they get there. Here the piazza isn't lined with colonnades as many squares facing churches are but with poplars. Between the rows of poplars is a meadow, famous for the three fat sheep that graze there weather permitting, an emblematic sight, indeed. Crowds gather near the bus stop, to gaze at what the diocese calls "The grazing of the sheep" that's announced by a church bell and on the radio to inform would be gazers that the sheep are in the meadow.

The sheep have created a cultural trend in our town. "*La Cloche*," The Bell, is what the people of Tournais now call the diocese, in recognition of the angelus bell used to notify them that the sheep are in the meadow. And, of course, there wouldn't be a popular name for the diocese without a double entendre - *cloche* happens to mean stupid, *clod* the Anglo-Saxons would say. Equally with poetic cynicism, they call the sheep, "*Les Condamnés de la Cloche*," The Condemned of the Bell, because of misgivings that the sheep are there just to be fattened for the bishop's table on feast days. People lay wagers on which of the three is fated to go next. In my notes I have this awful poem the newspaper *Le Soir* published about the diocese sheep back in 1938. I copied:

Love is in the meadow

Where the lambs, plump and tender, are made ready for the bishop's feast.

For one of the lambs, the bell shall toll, and the shepherd, to his tower, shall stroll.

To obtain his blade, poised for the lamb's tender throat. In hidden folds, fattened for the bishop's table.

Easter, Christmas, Epiphany reside, their secrets veiled, their mysteries implied. Each occasion, a treasure, waiting to be revealed, in whispers and whispers, their wonders concealed.

Behold, the throat of the lamb, doomed and bare, unveiled, a glimpse of fate's despair.

The sheep are not there this afternoon, probably because of the rain that's bending the poplars.

To cheer her up, I tell Mària that the poplars lining both sides of the piazza of Notre Dame de Tournai are curtsying to us left and right to indicate that Father Brabant didn't see anything thanks to the rain. "*Bonjour, bonjour gentilles petites filles*," they seem to say. She refuses to accept my assumption and answers that they look just like the poplars in Claude Monet's *Trees in Grey Weather* we saw with our art class

Tuesday morning at Le Musée des beaux-arts de Tournai. While admiring several Monets, I told her that my mother had taken me to the northern French village of Giverny less than fifty miles from Tournai to see Claude Monet's garden and home. The poplars in the painting were gone then; Monet, the guide told us, had sold them for lumber in the fall of 1891. Whenever I speak of my mother, Mària puts my head on her shoulder for comfort and kisses me deeply.

The poplars here seem anxious; they desperately want a respite from the fatigue the rain is causing them. Me, it's Mària's newest apprehension I want off our backs. Perhaps I also hope that something will happen and we'll have to cancel the appointment Mària made for us with the father and postpone judgment day.

The tonsured monk is at his little desk; this time, he's reading a brown leather-bound book whose title we can't see. He has a candle on the desk today for a bit of light the yellow stained-glass window above his head won't provide in this grey weather.

Father Brabant comes to the foyer to meet us, and I notice as soon as he walks in something different about him. His eyes don't go immediately to Mària like the last time. In a flash, I understand why. Mària senses it too, and both of us know that at least he suspects something. As agreed, unless he brings up what he thinks he saw, we won't.

We follow him to his office, where he asks us to take the seats in front of his desk. He sits behind the desk.

"Yesterday, the Vatican recognized the Franco government," he tells us as if that was the only thing weighting on his mind, and he is impatient to speak to someone of his disappointment. He may be disappointed, but he speaks with a straightforward self-assurance; and I think it's a trick. He or the diocese wants to provoke a reaction from us to find out where we and perhaps our families stand on the Spanish Civil War that since July 1936 and has been a burning political issue that's dividing Belgium. However, before I act on my deduction, Mària has mouthed herself into the trap: "Why is the Vatican supporting a fascist anti-democratic dictatorship?" she asks heatedly.

Mària who was the embodiment of caution telling Mother Bertrande her life's story is now back at the diocese, a sixteen-year old avenging angel against Franco of all people.

Every day, the Spanish Civil War is front-page news in Belgium. Even in little Tournai, we have violent clashes between partisans of the Spanish republican government and supporters of General Franco. Our school, like the country, is split along Belgium's left-right political divides, and fights between teachers are frequent. The students? They don't brawl but echo the views of their parents or teachers. Not Mària, of course. Not only is the spirit of contradiction too strong in her for that, but she's being nudged by Mr. Faure, our modern social science teacher and a fiercely partisan of the communist's cause. Being herself another *Passionara* of the left-wing Spanish republican government against the right-wing monarchists, Mària's at the forefront of the controversy at our school, driving me crazy with her little-girl habit of sticking her tongue out at people she disagrees with. In this too, she's quick with that gesture. When it's not her tongue she sticks out it's the Italian arm she gives to her opponents, accompanied by the discharge of a strident *"vaffanculo"* from her perfectly shaped mouth.

Sister Vaffanculo is one of the many names for her at our school.

Like the Belgian volunteers who trekked to Spain in support of the republicans, she'd have gone to Catalonia too had she found a way to go. As for me, I don't recall having any great interest in the Spanish civil war outside of Mària's support for the republican loyalists. But I do remember thinking then that there was something odd about that far away war. It didn't feel like you were watching a real war. It felt more like you had gone to the theater to see a play about a war and all they showed you were actors walking back and forth on a wide stage, rehearsing their lines and gestures; and you had to come back later and pay once more to see the actual show with the promise that it would be worth every franc.

Father Brabant has a queer look on his face. It's a look of surprise mixed with pleasure, and he tells Mària: "I don't know why I should be surprised, given that I have this warped conception that beautiful people are always on the right side of a question. So, I'm telling myself that no one who looks like you can be other than sympathetic to the republicans."

Even priests hit openly on Mària. She's long ago become numb to men and women hitting on her. But it makes me furious.

"I'm unhappy that the Vatican is supporting Franco," Father Brabant continues, "but I understand why. After all, Spain is the most traditionally Catholic country in the world, and Franco has made his rebellion against the government a fight against anti-clericalism and communism. Moreover, the church couldn't support a side that has banned me from Spain because I am a Jesuit."

In his demeanor, tone of voice and in what he tells us, Father Brabant talks to us as if we were adults, something he didn't do last Thursday; and I recall thinking that it's what he thought he saw in the rain that's making him treat us like this. Being old enough for sex, has conveyed grown-up status on us. It's a thought that comes into my head with no effort whatsoever. Mària contemplatively looks at Father Brabant.

She is as intuitive as I am and thinking the same thing, I can tell, watching her get angry that he hasn't come out with an accusation has reawakened her smoldering anger. What, however, has held her back from saying irritably to him, "Will you speak plain father" is that what he told us marks him as independent of the fascists. From her point of view that's significant because 1938's Belgium is also divided between those who have taken for granted that Mussolini and now Hitler represent the future and the socialists – communists who look to the Soviet Union not only to defend us against the fascists but to create a new egalitarian social order.

As if he's on an agenda with wings, Father Brabant switches countries and travels from Spain to the Congo in a single swoop. "The diocese has asked me to go to the Congo," he says in a quieter voice and in a way that makes us feel like friends he can trust. "Once there, my life's work will really begin. I've been waiting for this for a long time, you know. I'll be gone in a few months. I hope your aspiration to become renunciants leads you there in a few years. We all have personal feelings that no one who has not held the hand of another in pain can fully understand. My personal feeling is that we've an obligation to the Congolese people for the treatment Leopold caused to be inflicted on them."

I have no clue where he's taking us with these revelations. Maybe it's a prelude to telling us what he thought he saw us do last Thursday. But maybe it's a message that he has no problem with us; he is open-minded and understands. I can confidently say that Mària isn't giving him the benefit of anything resembling a doubt and may blow up at any minute for being taken for a mouse to his cat. I'm hoping he'll talk a while longer, so we can figure out how open-minded he really is. To that purpose, I ask him, "Is it your suggestion that the order of the Perpetual Cross is best suited, then?"

"Yes! Because The Perpetual Cross' focal point is *the least of these* and is concentrating its efforts in the Belgian territories of Africa: Congo and Ruanda-Urundi. It's there that you'll be allowed to do the most good, where you'll have the freedom to do what's best for the people. You won't have to defend or promote any Belgian imperialism if you don't so choose. There's nothing more important for the two of you than to be free to be yourselves. If you go anyplace else, the order will look too closely over your shoulders, and you won't realize the full potential of your calling."

I appreciate these admirable, selfless thoughts. By expressing the value of personal freedom and authenticity, it seems like he's indicating his support for us. I glance at Mària, to confirm my reaction with a smile. To my amazement, the Garboesque face is pale and more chiseled. I know that something the father said has made her even angrier than she already was. Brilliant Mària sometimes thinks with impetuous ears and is about to go hard on Father Brabant regardless of the consequences. For a split second, I hesitate; my mind is telling me that when she affronts him, it will put an end to the convent idea for good, and I will be spared. But entering the convent is in her blood; to lose it now will crush her, and who knows what a Mària who sometimes thinks with her ears may do. I don't want her to die; she means so much to me that I can't risk anything like self-harm.

"Excuse me, father," I say suddenly, "I'd like a word with Mària."

I don't wait for an answer. I grab Mària's right arm and pull. Shocked, she lets herself be pulled from her chair; and I take her to the door, open it and step out into the hallway where the groaning sound from the poplars bending under the persistent downpour reaches us and we both look up mechanically at the glass close to the ceiling. She then looks at me as if I have lost my mind. I continue to pull, to take her away from the glass to where we cannot be heard; where I'm sure we're alone in the diocese's hallway.

"I looked at you," I whisper, "and saw that you were getting angry. I didn't know what you were going to do."

She looks at me dumbfounded. For a moment, that's all she does; then she puts her arms around me, and her hand goes to caress my left breast, before squeezing it. "I love you too, she whispers breathlessly in my ear," and we go back in Father Brabant's office. My breast is burning, but I'm happy she squeezed it.

We take our seats in front of the desk. "Thank you, father," I say and nothing else.

"Don't mention it," he answers. "You guys are about the most mature sixteen-year olds I will ever have the pleasure to know. I really hope you'll consider what I told you about the

Congo. There's no place you'll have this opportunity to serve God to a more beneficial extent than there."

Chapter 6

"Tell us about the Congo, father," a calm Mària says, as if she were in our history class.

Without hesitation, Father Brabant speaks about the Congo as if it were his most treasured duty, one he looked forward to doing first thing in the morning.

"There's a European concept called *res nullius,*" he begins dramatically, like a person intending to make a lasting impression on an audience. "It means nobody's thing, the theory that items free of legal ownership are free for the taking. In 1878, King Leopold II of Belgium applied that concept to people and land in the middle of Africa the size of Western Europe, Belgium time seventy-five, for his personal use. Ivory was in great demand then and with rubber later he amassed a personal fortune. Millions over there died working in the rubber plantations of his private park. The *Kongokonferenz* held in Berlin in 1884 legitimized *res nullius* in Africa and gave other Europeans the notarization to do what Leopold had done. Thirty years into Leopold's rule, Belgium was so embarrassed by his brutality it took the Congo away from him. The Congo is the classic case of man's inhumanity to man, and a refutation of Christ's first commandment."

In the past, kings and cruelty went together. But in 1938, our king, although named Leopold too, attended a seminary in California and was hardly the Leopold in Father Brabant's account of the Congo. I wondered, therefore, what pertinence that story could have to a prospective postulant like Mària, unless it had something to do with the church itself.

After a brief moment of uncertain reflection and trepidation, I break the silence to ask what seems to me to be the most pertinent question: "What does that have to do with the church over there?" I steer clear of mentioning Congo as it evokes a sense of unease within me. I'm not sure, to be honest. Just like Mària and the street where she lives, the name of this place fills me with unease, sending shivers down my spine, much like the feeling I get when preparing to visit my mother's grave in the winter.

Oddly, Father Brabant seems taken aback by my question, and he turns his chair to the right, away from us, as if looking to the rain thrashing the window outside to save him from having to answer. He raises his eyes to the ceiling when there's no response from the downpour and remains immersed in his thoughts for a long while.

"Yes, yes," he then says resignedly, "there's much role of the church in what the Belgian state has done in the Congo. But that's not unusual. I am worried that the Congolese might not differentiate between the Belgian government and the church, leading to a strong animosity towards both. I view the church in a mechanistic manner, rather than an organic one. My primary concern is that the church may be perceived as yet another European colonial institution –"

Too soon, Mària interrupts him. "But what's the role of the church," she asks. "What are we doing over there?"

Father Brabant smiles at Mària's use of the pronoun "We" and for saving him from taking his idea to its logical conclusion.

"Yes, yes, our role?" he answers. "I am coming to that ... it's to evangelize like the apostles we are; make Christ known in order to save souls. We do that. Unfortunately in our eagerness to fulfill that mission, we compromise ourselves and do what Christ told us specifically not to do, serve God and Mammon at the same time."

The father may be pleased, but I'm annoyed at this use of the "We," and I'm looking for an opportunity to give balance to our visit here today. When he pauses, I quickly outpace Mària in asking the next question,

So, you're saying the church has fulfilled its obligations." But it has undermined its own integrity by catering to conflicting interests. How has it lost its integrity? One thing you did say was compromise.

"Very simply," he answers. "The church has found a way to benefit by appointing one of its members to oversee the colonies. It's easy to see the advantages of being accountable only to church rules and administrative centers that the church has established. It's interesting how religions often spread and influence other religions, cultures, and so on. And there is no legal prohibition, whether on a international scale or otherwise, against that. Churches offer numerous benefits. "The church has discovered a method to profit by appointing one of its members to supervise the colonies. As you can well imagine there're huge benefits to the church having the colonies accountable to church rules and administrative centers. Religions, as a matter of course, colonize other religions, cultures and what have you. And there's no law, international or otherwise, against that. Churches have all the advantages.

The Church of England, for example, benefits from having England as the colonial power in most places in Africa. With that monopoly in hand, England profits from the church's evangelization of the Africans. Colonization is made easier by having a population eager to worship like Englishmen do."

When he pauses, Mària, unpredictable as ever, belts out a laugh. Not a nervous chuckle, but an honest belly laugh. She has traded anger for mockery. Father Brabant's face turns crimson red; he's embarrassed that a sixteen-year old girl isn't taking him seriously and is brazenly showing it. Unfortunately, he presses ahead, having put on a brave sheepish look and a smile for a clunky answer,

"You have to give me at least some credit for my restraint in not blowing it out of proportion or adding unnecessary drama," he tells her by way of an apology. "The truth is that since the beginning of time, occupiers and other colonial powers have imposed their religion on conquered lands. It's a strategic and spiritual obligation they have. You didn't laugh when I told you that one of our principal functions is to evangelize the world. Anyway, if you remember anything of what I told you today it's that if you become a renunciant and go to the Congo, I hope Christ's first commandment will be your guiding light there as well. The greatest of all sins is disdain of others. To the narcissist, the Lord said, "Whores will precede you into the kingdom of heaven."

The high esteem Father Brabant seemed to hold the Congo was encapsulated in that speech. Over time, I would come to understand the deep pain that the Congo was inflicting on his soul, as he carried the burden of guilt for Belgium's actions in the region. However, I realized too late that for him, being a priest wasn't about striving for perfection or serving as a mediator between people and the Trinity. His primary and genuine purpose was to rectify the injustices inflicted upon the Congolese.

Liberating what Belgium had conquered was his goal. What he created, and what he believed in would have been his business, and that would have been fine with me if he hadn't succeeded in hoodwinking Mària. He spun stories about the Congo in her mind. He turned the Congo into the unique spot on earth where she could fulfill the Lord's call to do for *the least of these* as she would for Him. To a weirdly devout girl like Mària, the saying, "Whatever you do for one of the least of these, you do for me," was the highest order.

I told her what I had surmised: "Father Brabant has conceived a diabolical plan to lure you to the Congo."

But it was for naught; my wrought conclusion didn't move her because it was overly dramatic. In any event, she was trapped in the correlation between the Congolese *least of these* and the saying "Whatever you do for one of the least of these, you do for me" to be impressed by my histrionics about Father Brabant's luring her to Africa for his personal agenda. Eventually, going to the Congo took over her life and became her most important goal.

Miserably, her dream of becoming a nun fit in perfectly with the Congo. With the benefit of fifty-five years of hindsight, we can see that Mària was the renunciant who gave up everything and ended up in Africa to do Father Brabant's act of atonement for Belgium's sins in the Congo. What she found was misery.

I assume that Father Brabant is through instructing us because he should know that sixteen-year olds resent lessons. Lessons never do anything other than make them uncomfortable. I am about to be relieved that he hasn't taken retribution on Mària for embarrassing him when, unexpectedly, he starts to talk again and I think I know what's coming.

"Also," he says, in a measured tone, like in a sermon, "take yourself seriously, but don't overdo it or you'll sin the sin of narcissism."

Mària and I sit like statues in our chairs. That's what we agreed to do if he brought up the overhang. In Mr. Faure's modern social science class, we learned that a cold silent stare is all that's required to avoid mistakes. And we do that too.

"You should seek and be proud to have love of another in your lives," he continues; "love is the only means to commune with God. In the absence of love, an objective human species that is governed just by the will to exist is as devoid of life as a desolate and lifeless wasteland. But true love is impossible if narcissism is in the way.

"Man doesn't have the wherewithal to grasp the meaning of his own existence. Unable to acknowledge his ignorance, he chases absurdities, trying to make sense of who he is. Failing, he falls miserably into admiring himself. God, however, hasn't left man like a dog without a bone, destitute against the unknown; he's given him love to communicate with him. That's why I'm warning you against narcissism."

For a moment, it's Demosthenes we hear and Saul of Tarsus we see, and we stare back at him without a word. He chuckles nervously; then dismisses his chuckle with a wave of the hand, as if sorry he's put himself in a position where he feels uncomfortable and cornered.

"I'm sure you know Ecclesiastes 3:1, There's a time for everything." When he says that, Mària twitches; and I wonder whether he's not referring to hearing Mària scream in the overhang. It will take us years to realize that Father Brabant was, at heart, an old fashion sentimentalist. In the meantime, I curse to myself with all the rage that's within me and remain outwardly calm.

He is weary of us now, Father Brabant is, for we are far from what he expected, especially Mària whose approval he's doomed to crave. To get away from a subject he's probably sorry he brought up and compound the contempt he assumes Mària feels toward him – and that may also bring heated or derisive anger from her, he asks us if we'd like to discuss options as regards to convents in Belgium. He speaks cautiously and makes more hand gestures than usual, to help him in his new effort.

I sit back and watch Mària make the most of his having pissed her off with his soliloquy about narcissism. Her silent anger is what he gets, and he fidgets uneasily. Mària's understanding of men is a marvel of instinctive psychology.

But while she's expressing her anger with silence, it's my turn to move this meeting forward.

"OK," I tell Father Brabant with a smile, which causes Mària to give me her furious look; then to turn her face so that the father cannot see her stick her tongue out. "Please tell us about religious orders. You know so much about us now." I tell him.

For the rest of the appointment he talks only with me about the most appropriate order for our vocation. I'm a little lost because he's assuming that I'm like Mària, committed to a renunciant's life, and he excitedly asserts that the Perpetual Cross is unsurpassed, but admits that's because he's partial to the Congo where he hopes we will end up. The Perpetual Cross, he tells us, has laid claim to the Congo with their focus on *the least of these* and on having strong organizations in health, education, and administration. He's not telling us anything Mother Bertrande has not told us already, but he's doing a better job putting us in the context of the order and their objective. I, for one, like him better in the role of mentor than I do Mother Bertrande. I'm also thinking that, if necessary, we will be able to use one against the other once I'm convinced I can live with the convent that Mària has set her heart on entering.

Mària is not participating in the conversation, but I can tell by the way she pushes her hair behind her ears repeatedly that she's interested in what Father Brabant is saying about Perpetual Cross and *the least of these*.

I'm as stressed as a chocking person by whether or not to follow Mària. It's in the form of a lump the size of soccer ball in the area of my midline, and it's unbearable.

Following nine o'clock mass last Sunday, we met with Mother Bertrande outside of Notre Dame de Tournai's sacristy. She can tell that I'm stressed and when I answer truthfully why, she's understanding in a sympathetic way. However she continues to focus her attention on Mària, and on our way back home, to ease Mària's mind, I tell her that whatever Father Brabant saw us doing Thursday in the rain he hasn't told Mother Bertrande about it. If he had she would've behaved differently toward us today. We have a fight after that, when I ask her in frustration, "What is it about you?" as I've asked countless times before to force some of my frustration on her. She usually lifts her shoulders in the I don't know gesture. This time she takes it as an accusation and we argue over what she calls "This infernal thing."

Her blaming "This infernal thing!" is making me wonder if it isn't another manifestation of her becoming more religious; not in the sense of spiritual, but in the sense of dogmatic. She believes that because she has taken steps to answer the call of the convent, she must become a sanctimonious stinker in 1938. It was hard for me to look upon her as a zealot, and I told myself it was a phase brought about by the excitement at being fought over every Thursday and Sunday by Mother Bertrande and Father Brabant. Perhaps she was like all new converts succumbing to religious zeal for being chosen. Mària's phases, however, had the tendency of staying put, of not ever going away.

I bring her sanctimony up because I have in my January 1939 notes that she praised Tomas de Torquemada during the lecture on Christopher Columbus and Queen Isabella of Spain in our history class, taught by Miss Teitelbaum. Like me, all Mària knew of Torquemada was what we read in Dostoyevsky's *The Grand Inquisitor* for our literature class in the spring. Father Brabant had told us about it, and Mària insisted we read it in our world literature in translation class. Our teacher, Mr. Valérie, of course complied as he did when she asked for *Heart of Darkness* by Joseph Conrad and was reprimanded by the headmaster. Miss Teitelbaum didn't know that. When it came to Mària, all she knew was that she was an angel in mind and body descended from heaven as a favor to mankind. And here was Mària praising an historical figure famous for prosecuting non-Christians like her. It was as if Miss Teitelbaum had discovered that day wasn't day but night, and she completely lost it, bursting into tears at Mària's extolling of Torquemada. Like a disillusioned lover, she then accused Mària when she had regained some composure of being a "no principled juggler of ideas, who didn't care a hoot about anybody." Shockingly, all Mària could think of doing was coolly start lecturing Miss Teitelbaum on *The Grand Inquisitor* by Fyodor Dostoyevsky. A look of terror came over the teacher's face? What in the world? I wondered. She wasn't just a mouse, she was an hysterical one.

Miss Teitelbaum ran out of the class to the jeers of the students. Anti-Semitism had always been a monster awaiting little children at the end of town. By 1934, the monster had moved into the town center and some of the students took the opportunity of the teacher's distress to invite him inside the classroom. They applauded and one shouted, *mensengemeenschap*, something in Dutch about the German race and gave the fascist salute that was also now very much in vogue. That got to Mària, and she ran after Miss Teitelbaum in the hall. I remained in the class stunned and silent; then I wrote the event all down.

Mària a Tomás de Torquemada? Did I really think that in 1939? Sixty-two years later, it's so outrageous there's no sense in saying I'm sorry to Mària, who from heaven is watching "*La Folle de Tournai*" write these lines sitting propped up in her bed on Jerome's pillows in suite 209, at Maison St Jean, the very suite that saw my aunt go face the Maker on November 5, 1949 on the wings of a batch of sleeping pills she had amassed for a year.

The problem is that I didn't understand Mària sometimes. I say "sometimes" because I'm embarrassed to say a great deal of the time. Where did her ideas come from? She showed me a photograph once of her dressed in every detail as a miniature nun when she was six years old. It wasn't an amateur photograph taken in her garden but one done by a professional in a studio. Families went to studios to note special events like a first communion or the consecration of one of their own as a nun. "Mària, you were six years old. How could they do that to you," I asked her. I wasn't surprised at all, when she said, "I asked them for it."

Chapter 7

With Mother Bertrande's and Father Brabant's delighted assistance, Mària is a star enmeshed in the activities of the Tournai diocese. I can look on, petrified, as she's being carried to their destination at what I consider a breakneck pace. She's thrilled by their assistance and the prospects they promise. Father Brabant's sermon about the Congo is like a tourist brochure for the promise land. Mària takes me with her, and as we ride, I feel like one of the small logs that the river Tescaut, which cuts through Tournai, carries all the way to the coast and then across the Atlantic to the Congo. I still don't know about being a renunciant, but I'm hypnotized by the recruitment procedure of the time. More importantly, I cannot imagine not being with Mària ever. Spellbound I let myself be carried along to the Atlantic and to her promise land across the sea to the west coast of Africa below the equator. Regardless of the arguments we have, we continue to give ourselves to each other with the blind fervor that only trusted love can proffer. And I go with her. Unless you subscribe to the notion that you're not master of your emotions, being in love is an act of unreasonableness to the point of self-destruction.

How does one get out of the way of suicide or love?

The ultimatum follows inevitably. *"Qui m'aime, me suivre,"* if you love me, you'll follow me, Mària says to me following our session last Thursday with Father Brabant, as we are opening our umbrellas before stepping out into the rain to go to the bus stop. She says it flippantly, as though, well aware of its meaning. It's the last chance to get on board the train of her life.

I remember the feeling in my stomach that made me sick and the argument that ensued. Unfortunately, it was not one where reason had a chance to prevail. One goes where love is; what's the sense of anything otherwise? As the Trinity is my witness, that's what I felt back then: The only way for me to live was to sacrifice my life.

We are at the proverbial crossroad. Later in her room, love is unbridled. She bites my hand that I put over her mouth to stop her scream so hard that I shriek in pain. As if a servant possessed, Little Marie knocks frantically on the door; and Mària, infuriated, shouts, *"vas t' en, merde,"* get the fuck off. And later berates her for hanging around her door.

As if on commission, Father Brabant on Thursday afternoons and Sister Bertrande on Sunday mornings compete to encourage Mària's fervor. They take me along in mentoring her, showing her off, and finding sisters mostly from the *Perpetual Cross* order to put her in touch with for guidance and more influence.

In 1939, I catalogue the whirlpool of influence Mària is in so that I can slow down her plunge and mine into the unknown. That's my priority: Figuring out where the pressure points are so that I can be the one to have the most sway over her. My task would have been simpler if it had been only Father Brabant or Mother Bertrande motivating her. Unfortunately, there were also unfamiliar others like Albert Schweitzer[1], for example, the Franco-German multitasked humanist. Schweitzer[2], a physician, was laboring madly at a hospital in Lambaréné[3] Gabon in French Equatorial Africa. He too was

1.   http://en.wikipedia.org/wiki/Albert_Schweitzer

2.   http://en.wikipedia.org/wiki/Albert_Schweitzer

atoning for the historic offense of Europe's colonization of Africa. Father Brabant and Mària discussed Schweitzer constantly and formed between them a Schweitzer admiration society. Father Brabant cleverly used Schweitzer's works and faith to manipulate Mària into believing that she could redress what Belgium had done in the Congo and be the Belgian Albert Schweitzer[4]. All she had to do was follow his example and go over there. Was Mària so impressionable that she thought she could become Belgium's Albert Schweitzer? She never said out loud that her goal was to follow in his footsteps. That was too farfetched; people would think her *gestoord,* mad. However, she went about studying him and his work in Lambaréné with the fervor of one so infatuated with an idea as to be convinced her salvation depended on fulfilling it. She memorized passages from his books; and, with Father Brabant's assistance, even learned to play the organ at Tournai Cathedral because Schweitzer[5] was a famous organ virtuoso. Using Schweitzer[6]'s technique, she became a competent – if loud – organ player after just one year of study. Her Bach's Tocata and Fugue in D minor at the Tournai Cathedral at vespers one evening was so over-the-top dramatic; filling the church with so much resonance that people in the cathedral ran out. Father Brabant laughed hysterically. But the bishop heard what had happened and asked that Mària tone it down. She took offense at the bishop's remonstrance and didn't play

---

3.   http://en.wikipedia.org/wiki/

Lambar%2525C3%2525A9n%2525C3%2525A9

4.   http://en.wikipedia.org/wiki/Albert_Schweitzer

5.   http://en.wikipedia.org/wiki/Albert_Schweitzer

6.   http://en.wikipedia.org/wiki/Albert_Schweitzer

there again. Thinking of it, I don't think she played anywhere again after that incident.

Regardless of the remonstrance, summer vacation is in a few weeks, and they arrange for Mària to spend a thirty–day retreat as a guest of the Perpetual Cross Sainte Marguerite convent in Liege. As an "excellent" prospect, they have in turn given me a summer job to remain in Tournai and work with the Perpetual Cross sisters at the diocese under Mother Bertrande's personal supervision.

I told Mother Bertrande of my interest in medicine and as efficient as a cuckoo she assigned Sister Pierre-Madeleine who had attended the Institute of Tropical Medicine's nursing department at Antwerp to work on me. Sister Pierre-Madeleine was going to tell me all there was to know about the Antwerp Institute of Tropical Medicine. It also happened that she opened my eyes on what a permanently lustful woman was. She's unforgettable and after three meetings with her, my appreciation knew no bound. Her last name had been Oiseau des Isles, Islands' Bird. That was her real name, to which she was well attached.

"My name is Sister Pierre-Madeleine, I'm number 1072 in the sisters' register," she would say. "Before being born again, it was Astride Oiseau des Isles."

Twenty-five years old, she was taller than we were, almost six feet; full figured and head-held-high confident. She also had unattractive hungry, very light brown eyes made more prominent by thick elevated eyebrows; and she gave off a pungent sweet body odor that made us gag. We didn't know what to do other than bear it, for she was the most keen to open to us the door of her well-informed mind about religious life. Mària was as eager as a colt to hear all her fascinating stories about the integrated, insular, and cohesive institution she pined for, as Sister Pierre was keen to tell them.

(I thought about her often when I was writing my notes over the years. What would she have divulged, if like me she had yearned to reach out to the world outside with what she considered I'm sure a compelling story? I'm sort of glad she died without giving an account of her life as a renunciant. Other than the humor, Ms. Hulme's account is more than sufficient.)

The handkerchief Greta Garbo uses in *Camille* for the tuberculosis cough scene is what gave us the idea what to do about the problem of Sister Pierre's stench. Before going into the diocese, we would stop at *Le Printemps*, a French department store on Rue des Orfevres, to soak our handkerchiefs in Coty perfumes. When we were with her, we took turn coughing and using the handkerchiefs for a sniff of perfume to cover her smell. Only that way, were we able to make it through our sessions with her.

At our first meeting, Sister Pierre goes after us like a bull after a muleta, as we take turns in the office where she's receiving us. I considered myself overly preoccupied with sex; but I didn't know what such a preoccupation really was until I met Sister Pierre.

I know something is up when she announces she will see us one at a time, the first sister to do that with us. I think, of course, it's because she wants to be with Mària alone. Why can't she talk to us together? She gives me an evasive answer, something to do with wanting to establish the magnitude of our vocations, and only one at a time will do that for her.

After twenty minutes, Mària comes out and gives me a wink and the OK sign. I was wrong, then. I go in, sit in the still warm chair in front of a desk, Sister Pierre close by, scrutinizing me, not saying anything. She's cautious; doesn't touch me, not even my shoulders, or say anything that may compromise her. What she does is radiate questions like a stove radiates heat, ascertaining whether I, the prospect, may be receptive to her the prospector. One can tell it's something she does: It's her mode of operation. In my case, I just sit unresponsive, radiating nothing back, my hands on my lap waiting for the trial to be over.

Satisfied, she goes behind the desk to sit down. The look on her face gradually returns to normal, and during that time I sense that she's wondering about me. Much later I recognized that she wasn't concerned with the individual or the love dimension of sex; only the physical part. She was a breathing coiled spring combing the universe for a body to release the tension sex was imposing on her. The constant horny nun, that's the name I come up with. I watch her features return to normal, while she's speculating about the girl sitting in front of her; then I cough, needing my handkerchief soaked in Mr. Coty's perfume to mask the gagging sweet smell coming from across the desk. When the picture *La Cage Aux Folles* came out in 1978 I thought of her. It's my favorite film after *Camille*.

Sister Pierre, is one of a thousand wheels within the intense renunciant recruitment wheel between the two world-war period. By the time I entered Maison St Jean's nursing home sixty-two years later, there were no more such wheels; and with the disappearance of the minor orders, the church is so depleted in Europe that it must call on laypersons – mostly women – to perform church services.

Not surprisingly, Sister Pierre's first question is about the appeal the vocation of a renunciant has for me. I tell her that it's a doctor that I want be and we discuss my ambition. She's friendly but professional, easy to talk to, and quick with reasonable answers. Human nature is what it is. That's my reason for never trying to explain what's due to plain old chemistry. Here, too, it's just chemistry why I like Sister Pierre. I feel more at ease with her than any of the other sisters I've met at the diocese and why I can tell her that, unlike Mària who's always been sure, I'm wondering whether I'm fit to be a renunciant. When I say that, she interrupts me with a flood of guidance about what tests I should put myself through before taking the closing steps to enter the convent. Then, like all the other sisters we've spoken with, she gives me her take on sanity. Whether one is mentally sound is the most important factor in becoming a renunciant, she insists. She says nothing about chastity, and I don't ask. I take for granted that the institution assumes one is chaste.

Following our peerless session with Sister Pierre, it's time for our regular session with the rain and the bus. Sister Pierre has put Mària in a raunchy mood, and as we open our umbrellas readying to step out into the downpour, she slides a hand down my lower abdomen and tells me, "If she didn't stink, I bet she'd have an octopus's tongue to die for," and runs to the overhang to wait for the bus.

The octopus was in *The Dream of the Fisherman's Wife*, a woodcut done in 1814 depicting a remarkable octopus engaging in an expert's cunnilingus on the wife of a fisherman.

We absolutely adored this woodcut created by a talented Japanese artist, Katsushika Hokusai. It truly stood out as our favorite piece of art.

courtesy of www.katsushikahokusai.org

We were devoted followers of the octopus, referring to each other as "my octopus" to affirm that we lived in the shadow of the octopus.

I followed Mària to the bus overhang, leisurely, my face a gift to the drizzle.

It's already the morning of June 3, 1939, Mària's parents drive her for the first time to Liege, one hundred and fifty four kilometers west of Tournai, for her thirty–day retreat at the Sainte Marguerite convent. It's been drizzling continuously for five days and the sunlight is the color that walls of old buildings take when they've been rained on for weeks. Mària is to be a guest of the convent. Not yet a postulant and under no obligation to an order, she's regarded as someone who has shown a determined interest in religious life and service. As importantly, she has the diocese of Tournai's unqualified support and is named a "transcendental" prospect. My uncle drives me to her house to see her off on his way to Hopital Saint Georges, where he is on duty that morning. We get there as she and her parents are coming out of their house. They look no different from the well-heeled Belgians departing for the south of France to go stroll on Nice's *Promenade des Anglais*. Like a statue, Mother Bertrande, arms folded inside the sleeves of her habit, is standing on the sidewalk, waiting. François, the Labienvenue driver, so old that I call him Mister, is struggling with her suitcase down the front steps of the house, while Mària, up at the door, is consoling a weeping Little Marie. Had Little Marie not been weeping, I probably would have, to the tune of, "It's drizzling on the town as it is weeping in my heart." But seeing Little Marie cry hardens my feeling against tears and I don't weep. Mària under her outrageous candy apple red umbrella is radiant and smiling as if she were going on holiday to the south of France; I, on the other hand, am angrily dejected that she's so cheerful.

Away from the others she hugs me, whispering in my ear, "*qui m'aime, me suivre*," if you love me, you'll follow me, which enrages me more and gives me the gumption to slap her hand that's moving toward my left breast. She goes over to Mother Bertrande to curtsy and be blessed. She murmurs "Thank you" then gets in the front seat of the car next to François.

As the car pulls from the curb, she sticks her tongue out at me and waves, and the Labienvenue party heads west for

National Road 7. Ponderously, Mother Bertrande comes toward me and I introduce my uncle to her. They exchange *groeten* as we say in Belgium; then Mother Bertrande announces that she'll see me later at the diocese and walks to her car. I go unhurriedly to my uncle's car for the short drive to the diocese for my meeting with Father Brabant this morning.

When something is fresh in your memory, it's child's play to bring it out, even after sixty-two years. The morning Mària left for Sainte Marguerite sparkles in my mind and I have no difficulty remembering the bewilderment I was drowning in following her departure. I asked myself then, does she expect me to follow and that's why she's not concerned? Or, is it that she doesn't care, since her path is set; and whether I follow or not doesn't matter. Other than bewilderment, what's my answer? Shamefully, I can only think of what Heloise told Abelard, "If I lose you, what have I left to hope for? Why continue on life's pilgrimage, for which I have no support but you, and none in you save the knowledge that you are alive, now that I am forbidden all other pleasures in you and denied even the joy of your presence which from time to time could restore me to myself?" Bewilderment is food for love and bewilderment must have eclipsed everything else for I don't recall feeling any other emotion then.

During the drive to the diocese, my uncle who usually prefers silence reflects on the person he thinks Mària is: "She'll never make it as a nun," he exclaims, addressing the windshield. "The minute she opens her mouth, they'll spot her as a communist. Maybe it's what the antichrist has in mind, a devil in Germany, and a communist in the Vatican."

At one of our discussions in the garden, Mària sealed her fate as a communist as far as my uncle was concerned when looking straight into his eyes she announced, "Christianity is faith in socialism; it's Jesus Christ's collectivism in French," she told him provocatively. "Christianity should therefore help us in the practice of socialism."

That statement offended my uncle and although a member of the POB, the Belgian Workers Party, that's more socialist than anything else ideologically, he told her that there was a contradiction between Christianity and socialism. However, other than "an intelligent position is better than a dogmatic one," he didn't say what the contradiction was. Mària and I knew that here like every place else the contradiction was simply being slighted by a sixteen-year old girl's making such a big statement.

"No," she told him dogmatically, "there's no contradiction."

"She's only a leftist, Tonton," I tell him patiently. "Because she doesn't like the fascists, and it fits the person she thinks she is. She is not a communist; not a totalitarian," I tell my uncle amiably.

He gives me the puzzled look of one who sees someone for the first time. "I didn't say she was a totalitarian, just a communist," he says a length.

I'm tempted to lecture him the way Mària would have, using what Mr. Faure, her favorite communist teacher, who's responsible for her more opinionated ideas, told us in class about the communists. My uncle is, however, my immediate defense against my aunt and her manias; and never forgetting that I'm a guest at his and my aunt's house, I'm afraid of offending him. So instead of saying anything that may turn him against me, I use the time left before he drops me off to wrap my new plastic headscarf over my head so that I won't have to use my umbrella when I get out of the car.

I'm a bit late for the ten o'clock meeting with Father Brabant, but I don't hurry and not only because I'm enjoying the sound the little drops make on my headscarf and the drizzle that's wrapping me like a warm blanket. Hearing my favorite sound so close lessens the uneasiness I feel toward the coming appointment, and I reassure myself that it will have no great influence on my life. Then, too, the woodpecker who inhabits the diocese's poplars is at work in the rain, battering one of the trees. I saw it once and was amazed that such a little bird could perforate a tree so loudly with its little beak like that. I think of his dedication to carry out what he was put on the earth for, and I am full of admiration. A feeling that I'm courageous comes over me at that moment and I hurry up.

In the foyer, the tonsured monk, whose name Mària found out is Mathieu from Charleroi, a miserable industrial town east of Tournai, looks as if he has just visited his hometown. He isn't reading today and doesn't need a candle on the little desk to fill missals with prayer cards. The falling rain gives the glow from the high-ceilinged yellow stain-glass window a dirty-orange color. Like so many things, I can only guess why he doesn't have his candle on the desk to help him with his work. For a couple of seconds, I'm tempted to ask him; but it's too trivial, and I may embarrass him. While waiting for him to greet me, I take the headscarf from my hair and fold it. In its sheath, I put it in my purse; but he still doesn't look up. As I near his little desk, his eyes remain on his work. No Mària; ergo, no greeting today. Her absence surrounds her presence.

Finally, his head lowered, he points in the general direction of the hallway where Father Brabant's office is. His ill black eyes would be staring out of their sockets if Mària were standing here.

I knock on the door of the first office in the hallway, and Father Brabant shouts to come in.

"*Salve!* Did you see Mària off," he asks when I walk in. "I thought of going to her house this morning but I had an emergency extreme unction. Mornings are always a bad time in Tournai," he tells me.

He then puts the album, *Tintin au Congo*, he had been reading on the desk. "Tournai is a strange town," he continues; "it's unlike Etterbeek, my last place; there people tend to die during the night. I understand the Congo is like that.

"This album, *Tintin au Congo,* is by Georges Remi, a friend of mine in Etterbeeck. He has no clue where the Congo is; just repeating the drivel he reads. *Le Petit Vingtième*, publishes his work under Hergé, the pseudonym I gave him."

"*Bonum mane ad vos quoque,*" I tell him in answer to his *salve* greeting. Then I take a seat across from his desk and fold my hands on my skirt. "Yes, I saw Mària off." I try to sound blasé. But I'm not successful here.

"You look like you've lost your best friend," he comments lightheartedly, as if jollity is all I require to cheer up." He then laughs. I have never seen him laugh before. Like Mrs. Labienvenue, he has rotten teeth and I wonder if like her he is affected by the blue fear of dentists.

He then points at a file on the desk. "I was looking again at your CV and grades," he says. "Your wanting to go into medicine is auspicious. With a CV and grades in science like that, the Institute of Tropical medicine in Antwerp will welcome you with open arms; and you can be with Mària, who's sure to go to the Sisters of the Perpetual Cross and to the Congo. So instead of going there with Tintin, she'll go with you."

"I've just passed my baccalaureate. It'll take seven years to graduate from the Institute of Tropical medicine," I answer.

"Yes, yes, I thought of that and looked into the two-year program in the nursing department connected to the Institute. We send sisters there all the time."

Skeptical, I ask, "There are no renunciant doctors in the Congo?"

"Yes, there are," he answers. "But not from the Perpetual Cross. Our doctors are mostly from the Missionary Franciscan Sisters of Marie. They run the Queen Elisabeth Clinic of Kalina in Leopoldville."

"It takes seven years for general practice in tropical medicine and three more to specialize in pediatrics. That's a long time." While I'm saying that, I realize that implicitly I'm admitting considering becoming a renunciant nun.

"When you're sixteen, anytime is long. However, it doesn't have to be seven years. Sister Pierre-Madeleine attended the Institute's nursing department. Talk to her."

Ready to run off, I thank Father Brabant and leave him to his *Tintin au Congo*, which he picks up when I open the door to exit the office. My next stop is Mother Bertrande's office to receive my assignment for the day.

There is color in the hallway. The rain must have stopped to let the sun peak out for its weekly ten minutes of shine. It's a sort of understanding rain and sun have above Tournai, regardless of my preference for downpours especially when I'm stressed.

I walk down the hallway to Mother Bertrande's office. I had accepted the offer of a summer job from the diocese and was assigned to work with her. My only condition in taking the job was that I not be assigned to fill missals with prayer cards like Father Mathieu. Today is my first day. I knock several times on her door but there's no answer. It looks like she hasn't returned from seeing Mària off.

I'm elated she's not here yet; that gives me time to go visit with Sister Pierre. I dart down the hallway, to go knock on the constant-horny renunciant's door. She has been completely forthright with Mària and me, answering our question about convent rules. At one sitting, she went so far as to discuss clandestine love affairs in convents with us; not just the historical ones like Heloise and Abelard, but the ones taking place in 1939. As is her wont, she pooh-poohs nothing. Lying on Mària's bed later that day, convent Rules are at the top of what we talk about. "The stricter ones like obedience, chastity, and humility are necessary to the functioning and survival of the religious community," claims Mària. "These rules support the community's focus on the collective and the spiritual away from the individual's trivial materialism." This is not surprising that Mària thinks that way; she has believed as long as I've known her in the collective and the spiritual, socialism and Christianity. Me, on the other hand, after hearing Mother Bertande extol and Sister Pierre catalog the rules, I am not persuaded. I tell Mària the obvious, "The rules seem devised to circumvent and if necessary eliminate human nature through the will of the convent. But since there's no wall high enough to keep nature out, they suppress it as best they can with manmade rules and restrictions."

Mària reflects a while then says, "Nature can't be denied, can it?" There is something close to fear in her voice.

"No," I answer, as forcefully as I can. "And trying to deny nature anything must be like denying a beach to the tide. That must be the most stressful job in the world. You know how horny you get sometimes and you can't wait to ravish me with your tongue. What are you going to do when it's against the rules to even touch yourself let alone touch somebody? Be another constant horny nun like Sister Pierre? The gate of an abbey doesn't erase memories or make people forget who they are. You don't come out the other side a different person. You are the same person, except for your job and the "forgive and forget" rules that were put in place to help you start a new life."

"I'm going to think of you and touch myself the way you showed me and pray a lot. In the dark everything becomes the same." When you're seventy-eight you remember when you were sixteen and you sigh. When we were sixteen, nothing resisted the broom of our ignorance; and no barrier was high enough against taking risks.

Sister Pierre's door is open and she is sitting behind her desk, facing the window, enjoying it seems the momentary sunshine. She turns around when she hears my footsteps and gets up to come hug me. She likes me or she's just using the occasion to embrace another human being. I feel sorry for her in a conceited sort of way, which shames me. I recall my mother's saying, "A lonely person is not a comedian in a show."

"Mària is going to be a sensation in Liege," she proclaims expansively, as she closes the door.

"She's a sensation everywhere she goes and has been since I've know her back in fourth grade," I tell her so that she will turn off the commiseration she seems to think I'm looking for.

She doesn't get it and says in a voice a mother will use to sooth a sibling resentful of another, "You'll be a sensation, too, once you make up your mind to join her."

She's going to chatter about Mària all day, unless I tell her quick that Father Brabant has suggested I talk to her again about the Institute of Tropical Medicine at Antwerp. A light goes on in her eyes and I sigh with relief that I've hit the button that turns her switch on. Like an automaton, she's going to reveal once more everything she knows about the Institute. She does all the talking; I do all the listening and the note taking while she paces the length of her small office.

Chapter 8

War is hovering over our lives in Tournai, and no one doubts it will swoop down and have its way with us at the slightest change in the European mood. Most importantly, as far as I'm concerned, war presses on where I should go like a milling stone on wheat stalks, forcing me to take the first step toward becoming a nun renunciant.

War? It was not going to be a war, not in the sense of conflict. It was going to be another invasion from the east, a German occupation and rule. Not a war. Even if Belgium professed neutrality or had the physical means to stand up to the Germans, like the French, it didn't have the spirit. That's the way it was then, the way I noted it then; not the way I see it through sixty-two years of retrospection and regret. Let me be blunter: if the Trinity Itself had told me then that the war would turn out the way it did; that the *boches,* the dirty Germans, were going to be beaten, I'd have hesitated to believe It.

As Tournai reflects on that summer, the impending chaos becomes the flavoring element in its everyday life. The impending conflict serves as the theme in every event. When sexual desire becomes an obsession, people start to worry that war is imminent, just like the animals in the stories you hear about who flee for higher ground when they feel an earthquake coming. I became obsessed with evading danger and finding a safe haven.

What the *Boches* were going to do next was fodder for the daily headlines since my fourteenth birthday, March 7, 1936, the day the *Boches* repudiated the Locarno Treaty and invaded the demilitarized Rhineland. That day, drivers parked at the side of roads and streets to listen on their radio to the minute-by-minute speculation about France's reaction and the predictions of who would be next when it became clear France had no plan to deter the German offensive. Every day, the newspapers splashed some hack's opinion about "German attitudes," and the Germans grew more mythically invincible when France did nothing.

The First World War had a degenerative impact on the generation that experienced it. Like my uncle, that generation came out of the First World War completely in awe of the Germans and had the surrender proclamation ready for when the *Boches* came next. *Deze Keer Zullen Ze Blijven Voor Altijd,* This Time They Will Stay Forever, read the headline that sought to foretell Belgium's future. Mr. Faure might tell us the Soviets would defend us; no one, not even Mària, his favorite student, who by now knew as much about communists as he did, took him at his word – the soviets were just as frightened of the invincible Germans as we were, I told her. Her response was to stick her tongue out salaciously.

And it follows that upon the *aansluiting* of Austria on March 13, 1938, Belgians swap defiance for survival, as they have swapped resolve for abdication. Other than some members of the Communist Party, there is no one left in Tournai who hasn't put the Germans on the white armored conquistador's pedestal. People are psyching themselves up for what's coming.

By August, the general *sauve qui peut,* everyone for him herself is on. Against the background of imminent war, Sister

Pierre speaks for a full hour about her experience at the Institute of Tropical Medicine at Antwerp. I listen because with me she's more than a diocese recruiter filling quotas; she's someone who has demonstrated friendship toward Mària and me, and she knows she can explain anything without fear that I'll think it a clever recruiting ploy and turn my ears off. Who else but a friend would tell me, "If you come in because you're scared of *boches* or scared of facing the world out there, you'll be disappointed." And this: "if you've lost control of your life, find it before you consign yourself to a life like mine." The downside to that friendship is that her explanations are tediously protracted. It's as if her life depends on talking to explain things.

Sister Pierre reveals to me today that I can go to the Institute on my own volition regardless of my convent ambition.

"Don't let anyone tell you you've to be a renunciant to attend that institute," she tells me. "You don't. The question is, what are you going to do with a degree in tropical medicine? It's almost useless in temperate Belgium. Mària will be making a difference in tropical Africa, and you'll have a useless diploma. I don't think you'll be able to stand it. On the other hand, by becoming a renunciant and going to the Institute, you cover all the stops, human and spiritual... plus being with Mària."

My surprise is that there's no mention of prayer, sacrifice, poverty and good deeds in Sister Pierre's peroration. That can be explained by remembering that here, she is speaking as a bureaucrat. Besides it is implicit where prayer, sacrifice, poverty and good deeds stand in the scheme of a renunciant's existence.

It never occurred to me to question her motive. She was, however, adamant that I not sign up for the nursing program but for the doctor of tropical medicine curriculum, which would require seven years of study with my baccalaureate S (science), followed by a residency in the tropics, most likely Africa. But my loins have their own mind and their tremors are doing my thinking for me. Not having Mària's tongue there is unbearable. I try not to think of what the weeks at the Liege convent are doing to Mària. Sister Pierre's probing eyes watch me like a starved fox a hatchling. It takes me a while to understand her eyes; and being inexperienced, I'm convinced she's about to proposition me. Providentially, Mother Bertrande is looking for me and knocks once prior to opening the door to her subordinate's office. Sister Pierre lowers her eyes forlornly and stands up.

"Father Brabant told me you might be here," she says, walking toward me, an examiner on an inspection tour. Dutifully I, too, stand up and tell her that Father Brabant said I should speak to Sister Pierre about the Antwerp Institute.

"You envy your friend, yes," she says as if talking to a child. "You belong together where *the least of these* are most in need of your youth and faith. A nurse in tropical Medicine will do nicely indeed," anticipating that the war has made everything a priority.

The war is the main concern, and everything revolves around how to get ready for it. Older people are accosted in the streets and asked how it was during the Great War. After a while they just go about their business, not answering. By now they know that those who ask believe with only one ear the stories those who live through it tell, preferring to surrender to their awe of superman Hitler, the conqueror who has arrived as they say like an idea whose time has come. Underneath this fascination with the Superman is capitulation: there's nothing they can do about Germany so they let themselves follow the inclination to join not only what they cannot defeat but what is a thousand-year unique opportunity.

A dark euphoria takes hold of the people: the world they know is to be razed to the ground, and no other but the master race is to build the new one. How can they let pass this inevitable world-changing event without expectation while waiting to get on board? But so far it's all an abstraction, a notion, until August 24, 1939, when reality imposes itself with the radio announcement that the foreign ministers of Germany and Russia have signed a nonaggression agreement. To minimize the brutality of the announcement or perhaps to make sure listeners are aware that the world has turned, the radio station plays a record of Mozart's Requiem following the broadcast.

Suddenly, it's all acutely real and people become deathly quiet as if stricken mute by having been choked by the new reality. Heretofore, the Nazis and the Communists were mortal enemies, but the Molotov-Ribbentrop Pact has disabused them, and Communist party members run around like dogs chasing their tails, saying all sort of crazy things to rationalize the pact and the new friendship between the Nazis and the Communists. The public parks resonate with speeches attempting to explain the Soviets' turnabout. All the same, the people regard Bolshevism as foreign and a greater threat than Nazism, although I doubt they could tell you why. Whatever it was, the Communists in the parks couldn't put a dent in the people's sense that Germany was the master of the world and the designer of the *New Order.* Pro-fascist paramilitary group sprang up as if Hitler had traveled overnight to Belgium to sow the seeds of his *nieuwe orde.* Mystification is an incredible thing; it's more than a fifth column, it's the 14th century Black Death, an influenza pandemic, a pathogen that depletes a country's spirit.

Mària's letter from Sainte Marguerite that day ghoulishly brings up the Germans in this context: "… and when the *Boches* come, the convent will be the safest place."

That afternoon of August 24, 1939, I tell my aunt that I'm thinking of following Mària to the convent in Liege following the Institute of Tropical Medicine at Antwerp that I've discussed with my uncle. She beams with pride, and at that moment her face is not witchy-pale yellow but pink. She will tell all her church cronies about her niece becoming a renunciant with a medical degree. And she'll be given even more status. Not only is her husband a physician; she's taken in an orphan who is repaying her debt by becoming a renunciant doctor. She will gain huge face and understandably her arrogance will be as huge. Her eyes widen in what I think is gratitude, and she looks as happy as someone like her can look happy. From now on, penances for sins of untidiness will be metered out in numbers of rosaries I'll have to recite. Whether I leave a glove on the sofa or spill something, the penance after I announce that I am considering entering the convent in Liege will be a multiple of two rosaries. Very soon, that also peters out and ceases completely when the Germans, the *sales boches,* arrive in Tournai.

"I told my aunt about the convent," I tell Mària, when she gets out of her parents' car upon her return from Liege. She takes that in as if she expected it. I'm furious; remain on the sidewalk, watching her go up the stairs into her house.

So as I must, I come to the question, would I have become a renunciant had I not known Mària? My answer is, no! Even if I had thought of it, convent rules and awareness of my sexual proclivity would have discouraged me. *Of course*, it's on Mària that I place the decision to take the closing step in becoming a nun renunciant. Was she my vocation's only impetus? No, she was not. There was also the chance to escape the coming war, and there was Father Brabant's clever handling of what he had learned about me. As importantly, there was my leaning toward a life of caring for the sick, a predisposition that was as powerful if less explicable. I would have gone into medicine; and, following the third meeting with Father Brabant, I looked into the possibility of enrolling at the Institute of Tropical Medicine in Antwerp, with the view of being where Mària would be without going into the convent. But in the end Mària was too much the alpha and the omega of my mind, heart and body; and as she had blinders on for the nunnery I followed her there. It's out of weakness that I became a renunciant. By default, one might say. Can anything be so simple? It is, if I tell you that I would have followed her to one of those Boches' extermination camps the newsreels played after the war if that's what it had taken to be with her. So instead of an independent doctor, a nursing renunciant is what I became. It wasn't a *heart having reasons that reason didn't know* thing. I knew in words written in awareness that who I was was the reason.

Surprisingly, being in a convent together solved great many things for us.

In time, Father Brabant, helped us with the formal application letters to Perpetual Cross. And he and the bishop wrote their own in support. Soon after, the Reverend Mother asked us in for tea to look us over. Then my aunt and Mària's mother came with us. By then, the hand-wringing was over, and we were on our way to the Perpetual Cross Sainte Marguerite convent in Liege to hide from the war.

When by February 1945 the Germans had gone from Belgium, and the Pathé Frères newsreels began showing what the *Boches* had wrought in Poland and other places, Mària was hit hard. For days, she didn't eat. Pale, she walked like a ghost in search of its physical form. Preoccupied with heavy thoughts elsewhere, she talked little. From the little she told me, I gathered that she was experiencing an acute case of what seemed to be remorse. It could've been shame; I don't know, really – a failure of some kind.

She turned to prayer with frightening zeal. My anxiety for her state of mind could find no outlet except in the idea that once in the Congo she would be free from the war and what was troubling her. Protected by apartheid and the colonial freedom to do with the natives what she wished, she would get well. As I turned to hope that Africa would free her from both her newly found zealotry and that cursed depression, Mària did the same for her own relief and joined me in lobbying all the people who admired her, from the Tournai bishop to our adored Mother Paul Saint-laurent-des-joncherets, the Mother

Superior in Liege, to hasten our departure. We couldn't wait to get to Africa.

Chapter 9

The vessel taking us to the Congo is named the Leopold II, a converted American partially refrigerated surplus liberty cargo ship that's returning to the Congo for more of the bananas Belgium has become fond of. I hesitate to speak of the canvas on which our departure is painted because it is dominated by only one color: grey, with a mosaic of all the hues that the affecting color grey enjoys with the help of clouds and the obligatory rain Antwerp is also known for.

On the roof of what must be a warehouse is an enormous billboard with "Do not believe that in Belgium it is always grey," written on it in gigantic letters.

Nevertheless, there's an agreeable wind from the west that blows with the stench of diesel; but I can smell a flower in many scents, and I tell myself it's the scent of a rose that's a little faded.

"How many renunciants you think have experienced this sight?" Mària, leaning next to me on the upper deck's rail, asks excitedly, her deep voice deeper, as the ship pulls away from the port of Antwerp and we watch my uncle, aunt and Mària's parents waive white handkerchiefs under black umbrellas below on the port's central pier. Everyone is synchronized in cheerful ignorance of what the future will impose upon us who are on a ship bound for the colonies. All thoughts of the people of these colonies – how they feel about being under Belgian rule, how they see us, or what they dream for themselves – are obliterated by the sense of self-importance of being Belgian masters. There're reasons one is a predator and consumer in chief. Masters don't have to worry they are strangers. No land is strange to them. Behaving self-importantly is proof of that truth. For me, however, it feels as if I am on an exile ship that will never sail back to Antwerp. I'd be dreadfully apprehensive if Mària weren't at my side. I wouldn't be there were she not at my side.

Fifty-five years later, supported by Jerome's pillows in my suite at Maison St. Jean, I think about that journey with love, until both love and the journey fade into fear of what's to come.

Mària exudes her dream to be on the journey, at the end of which her desire to uplift *the least of these* makes her an indication of the global push for progress, a catalyst for advancement.

Good will flourish wherever she stands on Congolese soil, like the mythical orchid that never fades. She'll feel that way whether I'm there or not. Fifty-five years later, I swear on my immortal soul that if she had known what was in store for her, she would have gone whether I was by her side or not.

Hope comes in many hues but always before everything else, the Congolese are fond of saying. Hope was what Mària was looking forward to in the Congo. But the Congolese, who also have an excessive fondness for lotteries, like to say when they lose, which is all the time, that "people think they're going to win the lotto but not die."

I wish she'd gone to California, but she was after *the least of these*, and *the least of these* were in dark Congo; not in light-blazing California.

She was a favorite of all our teachers because her blazing mind latched onto their ideas with an alacrity that frightened many of them. And she did the same with outsiders, sometimes faster than an oyster latches on an Ostend reef. That's what happened with the idea that the Congo was the one and only place for the type of renunciant she wanted to be. Father Brabant's salvation awaited him in the Congo and his passion for that land leached onto Mària's compulsion to serve. Was it a mistake because flying too close to the truth with wings made only of optimism she paid with her life? Like Icarus who ignored his father's plea, Mària ignored mine not to go too close to an ambush. Like Icarus's wings melted by the sun, Mària's dream dissolved by the truth of colonial Congo. Icarus fell into the sea and drowned. Mària entered the labyrinth of colonialism and used a noose around her beautiful neck to get out. The finishing insult was her being made a Knight of the Order of Léopold II[1] two years after her death for services to the Congolese people. Was Mària reckless because she didn't listen to me, hammering in her ears that we were embarking on a journey fraught with the dangers Icarus experienced?

"The horror, the horror" I would chant annoyingly to her, like we used to do back in Mr. Valerie's class; for everything I had heard and read about the Congo pointed to that colony and its people as dark-hole mysteries. No Belgian cared to be in tune with the cultural profile of the Congo. You might then ask, "How did the Congolese and we Belgians talk to each other?" The mean was oppression, both from the inside and from the outside. We both used the oppressor's language when we talked to each other. Mària thought she would change all that. "We're not deportees being banished but apostles, entrusted with the mission of making where we're going a better place," she'd say with quixotic optimism. "We'll do so

---

1.   http://en.wikipedia.org/wiki/Order_of_L%2525C3%2525A9opold_II

much, we'll be famous, we'll be modern Albert Schweitzers women. Win the Nobel Prize. I'm not overlooking the burden fame is, but praise the lord we find that kind of fame." I could never compensate for her being so odd. Deep down she must have been lonely.

In 1945, Africa was the only of the seven continents almost entirely run by foreigners from Europe. Naturally then, we looked at the Africans with superior paternalistic eyes. I have lived long enough to hear that it was offensive to have seen them through such eyes. Let me swear on Mària's bible that it was still the least distasteful of colonization's attitudes toward the Bantus. Be that as it may, Mària and I were not embarking on a *civilizing mission,* intending to make Belgians out of the Congolese. No! Not us! I was going to nurse them and Mària teach them to read. Mother Bertrande assured us "there was nothing wrong with being parents to those who needed mothers and fathers."

What did I note of our voyage to the Congo to be parents?

I noted the captain; not because he was lord and master of the Leopold II but because he was taciturn and had to be operated on for the most trivial information. Such people affect me greatly because they remind me of my aunt, which scares me. My aunt spoke only when she was angry. The taciturn middle-aged captain spoke only when drunk and only to insist on telling us wondrous tales of the Congo so that he could enlighten us about the Bantus who were in league with the devil communists, bent on cheating Belgians out of what was rightfully theirs. Had I not been there, Mària would have snubbed him. All the same, I made it so that we listened to him as little as possible and only when we had no other choice, at the evening meal, for example; and when we walked the deck in the late afternoon the first couple of days of the voyage. (Having noted that by then he was drunk, we changed the schedule of our promenade.) He was a Dutch Belgian aristocrat, a baron, the son of Baron Adrien de Nerval, famous for having led the very first Belgian expedition of 1898 to the South Pole.

Because he was an aristocrat, we were reluctant to accept him for the bore he obviously was. Stereotyping being what it is, we were invariably hopeful that the baron part of him would be greater than the sum of his prejudices against the Bantus. We waited for him to make a big show of the noblesse oblige we were sure he was born with. We should not have been so naïve. Here we were going to minister to the *least of these* and we were as naïve as the most commonplace idealists. In retrospect, that was a bad sign.

The distance from Antwerp to our destination, the Belgian Congolese Port of Matadi was 10,158 kilometers, 5278 nautical miles. Our captain calculated that his ship cruising at ten knots had a twenty-three day, a month less a week, journey on its horizon. Except for the few times when the sea was rough, the little liberty ship was comfortable in a stark sort of way. As the only renunciants on board, we had the sisters' cabin, located toward the bow of the ship to ourselves. The cabin was named in memory of Sister Alix, the martyr, who had embarked on the Leopold II for the Congo the previous year only to disappear without a trace in the Mbuti area inhabited by groups of Pygmies. It was idyllic having this little cabin to ourselves, its door reinforced with iron bars just in case a member of the crew decided to peek at the renunciants in their informal attire to entertain his mates with tales of Mària's beauty. The captain even came out of his reserve to tell us to lock the door. Once that door was locked, it couldn't be opened from the outside without an oxygen-propane cutting torch. The cabin had two large portholes that we kept opened to take-in the sunshine that burst in as soon as we left Antwerp. No surprise that we thought we were being blessed and declared the sunbeams an Isaiah prophesy.

The crew included the most deferential fourteen men we would ever meet. To be sure, they stared at Mària, when we came on board, except interestingly enough for the two members we saw kissing once during the voyage. We realized that was not a coincidence, and understanding why precipitated the first and only discussion Mària and I would ever have about our own sexual orientation.

Like seamen the world over, the crew members were religious men too; and every morning at six o'clock they gathered on deck for prayer followed by Mària's reading from her bible. It was not the sound of her beautiful voice that moved them so; they wouldn't have minded if she had the voice of a gilt. What they worshiped was Mària's intensity of feelings behind the words. When they think of angels, Mària is probably what comes to mind.

On October 14, 1945, the Leopold II docked at the port of Matadi that Henry Morton Stanley, famous for the question "Dr Livingstone, I presume?" founded in 1879 at the mouth of the great Congo River.

Mària stayed up all night waiting for the tugboat that was to maneuver the Leopold II into the Matadi harbor. I didn't and went on deck only when I felt the tugboat pull alongside us and heard the crewmen curse its skipper for his usual lateness. Mària was staring shoreward, saying *paternosters*, her face the color of the dawn. She was staring at her new land's wretchedness: the few wooden buildings all covered in rusting corrugated zinc surrounded by sparse trees of a grungy green color. Belgians were in khaki uniforms and colonial cork hats; Bantus were in rags. We expected the lack of infrastructure; after all this was a colony and this was Africa, but we expected the paucity and shabbiness of the buildings and their surroundings to be mitigated by an exuberant tropical sunshine. We had hoped for splendor in the landscape's wilderness to compensate for the lack of infrastructure. That's what we had hoped for to make the place joyful. Was that too much to hope for? But it was the drabness that hit me with a bout of dejection like a gunshot. If I had been offered a return voyage at that moment, I would have accepted, if only to ease the pain in the area of my midline in torment. And I was worried about the disappointment Mària must be feeling. I leaned against the rail next to her as we approached the Matadi harbor. She shuddered as she realized I was looking at what she was looking at and that no amount of joyful tropical sunshine could make up for the bleakness of what we were seeing.

"I'm sure Leopoldville doesn't look like this," she said challengingly.

"Yes," I answered. And left it at that, thinking it wise to let the Congo be discovered for itself.

The efficiency of the docking helped some, and we hoped that something else, anything, an unknown quality, a flight of birds of paradise, the sight of a magnificent silverback would emerge to alleviate our apprehension and improve our mood.

When it came time to disembark, Captain de Nerval came to our cabin to take us to the gangway where the crew members had assembled. As sons are to their mothers, many of them in tears, loathing saying goodbye to us; insisting on coming with us and carry our luggage to the train station. I would've preferred a journey by river barge to help reconcile my negative first impression of the Congo with what I had come there to do; unfortunately, the Congo River wasn't navigable from Matadi to Leopoldville due to the many falls and rapids from the Yellala to the Livingston Falls, the swiftest in the world due to its narrow channels.

At the station, the crew members stood around us sheepishly, hats in hand; then all at once, as if reminded it was Sunday, they all knelt to receive our blessing. Afterward they kissed their angel's hands and left us with waves and "we will never forget you" expressions of gratitude. (Later, I came to regard those "expressions of appreciation" as words of sympathy or condolences. Perhaps they knew like men of the sea often do what awaited us.) Now we had four long hours of waiting for the noon train to Leopoldville, and so we met Jerome, the first Congolese we had a conversation with on Congolese soil; and a taste of what relations with the natives were like.

He was an older man who stressed his age to make him trustworthy in our eyes, aware that Europeans did not trust pestering would-be guides. To cope with the suffocating humidity, I sought to remain immobile, but Mària pleaded that we take Jerome's offer of a tour. I agreed on condition that he take us to a cool place, as I couldn't imagine such spot in Matadi. Jerome's eyes lit up, and he announced ecstatically that we would find relief from the humidity he saw me suffering from in a cave. All of a sudden, he went from pestering "guide" to rescuer of two handholding-dazed nuns when he told us that he would take us to the Cave of Diego Cão[2] in the hill above Matadi to see what the Portuguese who were the first Europeans to come this way in 1485 wanted the world to know of their stopover here.

Mària consigned our luggage to the stationmaster and we left with our guide, heading west. It was a long walk, but we were rested from our month-long sea voyage and Jerome, who looked like he hadn't eaten in days, was a surprising font of information about Europeans' visits to the shores of the Congo. Listening to him soften the miles of rough and hilly roads. We reached what we then realized was Matadi's highest point as the town laid at our feet and the Cave of Diego Cão[3], where it was at least twenty degrees cooler than outside and no humidity. I'm sure O Senhor Diego Cão[4] and his men were as delighted in 1485 as Mària and I were in 1945 to enter this refreshing cave. On a boulder inside, chiseled deeply in the limestone, as the ancient Egyptians carved their hieroglyphics to survive eternity, Diego Cão's graffiti gave notice with the Portuguese flag and a cross as witnesses that the ships of King John II of Portugal had arrived in the Kongo[5]. Jerome

---

2.   http://en.wikipedia.org/wiki/Diogo_C%2525C3%2525A3o

3.   http://en.wikipedia.org/wiki/Diogo_C%2525C3%2525A3o

4.   http://en.wikipedia.org/wiki/Diogo_C%2525C3%2525A3o

translated Cão's 461-year old graffiti for us and recounted the story of the Portuguese stopovers on the west coast of Africa starting in 1482, marking their new African territories with stone pillars like the boulder. After a pause, he added with a smile and what I took for a regretful tone, "And now you nuns have come to make us even better Christians."

We were the only people in the Diego Cão's cave and we remained leaning on the famous boulder for over an hour listening to Jerome's fascinating tales of European visits and conquest. He couldn't read or write he told us and had learned the various accounts by memorizing the stories he heard while working as *homme a tout faire,* handyman, for archeologists, tour guides and tourists over the years. Politely we asked him if he wanted to tell us about his homeland. And when he said he'd be glad to tell us what he was aware of, we urged him on with the promise of a good tip. I was particularly interested in finding out if the war had changed the Congo, and I asked him to tell us what Congolese eyes were witnessing. In Tournai, Mària and I had spoken to several Congolese, but they were from a group Father Brabant was supporting, and either they were too apprehensive to be forthcoming or too eager to tell us what they thought we wanted to hear, which was that the coming of Belgians to the Congo was the answer to all their prayers. They were not lying or mocking us; only protecting themselves with an exercise in self-affirmation, having impressed upon their own minds that imperialism was God's gift to the Congolese. (We would experience a lot of that.) What a fascinating protective mechanism self-affirmation is!

5.	http://en.wikipedia.org/wiki/Diogo_C%2525C3%2525A3o

Thank the Trinity we were detached enough to understand from which pond these people were fishing from.

We needed objective answers to get psychologically ready for our quest, and we couldn't find them. Even nuns who had worked in the Congo were unable to draw an objective picture of what awaited us. The nuns who insisted on being overly benevolent portrayed the Congolese as childlike creatures (I'm reluctant to say noble savages); the embittered ones, on the other hand, had them all as liars. Then, there were the nuns who were so protective of their experience there they refused outright to discuss the Congo with us. They were like the survivors we talked to after the war. By September 1945 we had a sense that a predicament common to anyone traveling to strange lands was looming over us. Trembling, hugging each other for reassurance, as in an animated film, we told each other that good hearts and the Trinity's blessing would see us through our nervousness that couldn't be other than momentary. The humility pounded into our brains couldn't make us other than welcome wherever we went. God only knew the trials the Congo had in store for us.

Jerome was looking at me; not at Mària. That was a new experience. I took out my pad and pen from the special pocket in which we were allowed to carry personal things to note down his words.

Chapter 10

In 1945, Jerome's French was as approximate as the colors yellow and amber are to each other. What I wrote are perforce interpretations of what he said. Like a man who alters his hearing to cope with being blind, Jerome made up for his illiteracy with narration embellishment. His expository style was fit for a would-be stage actor. (I later learned that another of my judgments was incorrect. Jerome was from a family of Jalis, northern storytellers, and his way of speaking was actually part of his heritage and nothing to do with coping with illiteracy.) But he was a professional, and pleasing the customer for a fee was his métier. The first thing he said when he started to tell us what the Congo had become after the war was, "The Congo is running an exhaustive race with the Belgians and only God can tell which one will tire first. I'm betting on the Congo, for even the people who invented God cannot escape the destiny reserved for all occupiers."

When I finally understood what he said, I interpreted for Mària and we both winced that a sane person would teach a native to say such drivel.

"Don't tell us what somebody said. Tell us in your own words," Mària told him politely. "You speak beautifully, but our time is short." He did, and it was the finest introduction to the Congo we could have prayed for on our first day there. But time was passing (in Jerome's language "we were passing,") and it was time to return to the station. However shaken by the premonitions created by what Jerome told us about the Congo, the cool Diego Cão cave had refreshed us. We started down after a pause to look at the town and the docked Leopold II. Our friends were already loading up bananas into the refrigerated hold of the ship for the return trip to Antwerp. When we reached the station, we only had forty-five minutes left to wait for the train. I was very much taken with Jerome and his thoughtful nature (and would remain so for fifty-six years). After paying him generously for the tour and his insights, I asked him to remain with us until the train. That's when he said that if I ever needed a manservant, he would apply for the job. I could always find him at the Matadi station.

When we were boarding, he thanked us and said in his rough French the phrase that remained my storm lantern during my fifty-five years in the Congo, "Thank you for not treating me like a little person (child)." Mària and I were twenty-three years old.

The next day, Monday, October 15, around seven in the morning, we got to Leopoldville. I remember being tired after being on a train for 20 hours with bad seats, little water, and no food. Even though it's been fifty-five years, I can still remember the day as if it were just yesterday.

Of my fifty-five years in the Congo, the first two days in Leopoldville are the ones I remember minute by minute most clearly. Those two days determined what my life in the Congo would be.

Leopoldville, now Kinshasa, is situated south of the equator and subject to a tropical wet and dry climate in reverse order from what the northern regions experience. In October 1945, the wet season was just beginning and would last until the end of May at which time the cooler dry climate would, God willing, come again.

Reverend Mother Melchior – Mother Melchior was the Mother Superior in Leopoldville – and Father Brabant, the bishop's auxiliary, as promised, were waiting for us. Had Father Brabant not spoken, we would not have recognized him. Had we passed him in the street, we would not have known who he was – he had aged beyond recognition. His voice, white cassock and that Mother Melchior was standing next to him gave him away. He had grown a beard that was now grey. His stoop had not been there when he was mentoring us back in Tournai. Thick eyeglasses magnified tired or disillusioned eyes. He was now a poster for a colonial priest. Already in Leopoldville five years, he had left Tournai a couple of months following the German invasion of Belgium in May 1940. Rumor had it that he had joined the *Netwerk van de weerstand,* resistance network, and the bishop had shipped him to the Congo as punishment. Of course, that wasn't true. He had wanted to go to the Congo all his life and was pleased to leave Europe to its Second World War. He wrote to Mària in liege and me in Antwerp about his departure for Africa, and to bid us Godspeed with our studies; promising to be at the Leopoldville station to meet us when we got there whenever the Trinity willed it. He had brought two extra umbrellas, which he held at arm's length in front of him to remind us of home and the rain – and perhaps of our adventures during our journey in the labyrinth of the Tournai diocese. Once we had retrieved our two papier-mâché suitcases, he told the driver to take us to the diocese cafeteria. It was his experience that new arrivals were always starving.

After the drabness of the Matadi port, we needed Leopoldville to sparkle and expunge our dejection. We were, therefore, as eager as vacationing children are to find the sea to get a look at the capital of our new home. "Redemption is in Leopoldville," Mària murmured; and expectantly, we sought to experience fully the impact of our first impression of the city that had grown from a village also discovered by Henry Morton Stanley in 1881 and named in honor of King Leopold II of Belgium. I wrote down that anxiety was gnawing at us like the hunger pangs we were enduring. Like the children seeing the sea for the first time, we gawked out of the car's windows at what was happening in the streets, all the time beseeching the Trinity to make Leopoldville exotic if He must, but still a quaint provincial town. We looked in vain; the Trinity had chosen to make Swiss villages quaint, not Leopoldville. The Trinity had kept nothing quaint or provincial for Leopoldville. Instead, the Trinity had chosen to spite the sunshine and hang a foreboding gloom over the city. The streets reeked of deprivation as most wretched slums do. A deep sense of mourning washed over us. Unfolding in front of our eyes was what Belgian colonialism had produced here. I had no inkling of that then. Then it was just what was unfolding in front of our disquieting eyes, to create a cultural and psychological conflict in our minds; and from which we had to look away.

Mària, as pale as when she was going through her depression back home, was trembling as if the temperature had dropped. Nothing was at ease here. Everything was disquiet. The Africans used the streets for copulation, cooking, marketplace, bodily functions, pigsty and everything else humans engage in. It's not that we didn't expect something like this. In Tournai we were told often for a laugh that "They do everything in the streets." But eye-witnessing everything being done in the street as the most natural thing in the world on such a scale shocked us. The shock was in the details of what they did in the streets. Until we saw it, it had been another abstraction, part of what we had heard the Congo was like. Sure, it could not be *exactly* like that! After all, the Congo was on this planet.

Then, there were the people themselves. Those on the move, whether they had a load on their head, a child by the hand or on their backs, walked in slow motion. They seemed careful with each step they took, one foot hitching in front of the other, without lifting either foot, as if they were not sure where they were going, afraid perhaps that Henry Morton Stanley was waiting down one of the trails to do to them what he had purportedly done to their forebears. Much later, the sight of these people sleepwalking like that reminded me of the scenes in the newsreels after the war. Tellingly, when I make out those newsreels in my mind fifty-five years later, I see the Congolese with that bewildered look on their faces.The expression on the faces of people who were stuck with a weight about which someone had said, "Carry this and you will go to heaven." The expression of those on whom a joke was played.

Back on October 15, 1945, the Congolese as victim was as far from my mind as A is from Z. The heaviness that bestowed upon the people the forlorn expression that Mària and I witnessed upon our initial arrival in Leopoldville was a revelation that only dawned upon me in retrospect, as I retraced my journey through the Congo and reflected upon my role in the colonial enterprise undertaken by King Leopold II and Belgium in this region.

For years, I compared their lives and my mother's. Unlike my mother, who could not endure her life and ended it, the Congolese did not commit suicide. The church had transformed suicide into a malevolent act, condemning it as a pathway to eternal damnation, just as it had stigmatized homosexuality. After being fully bitten by Congo's reality, toward the end of my second year or so there, I couldn't help but feel a deep sense of sympathy for the Congolese people. It seemed as though they had no means, not even suicide, to escape their fate.

Father Brabant, sitting next to the driver was commenting on what the car was passing by and on how life was lived in Leopoldville's *cité indigene,* the Bantu sector. Leopoldville was the capital of the colony seventy five times larger than Belgium. Belgians were proud that India was only fourteen times larger than Great Britain.

Father Brabant began to tell us about life here and announced, "The Bantus call us Mbulamatadis, rock blasters, behind our backs. It's fascinating, absolutely fascinating, how they transmute one characteristic to classify the entire Belgian race. That's the oral tradition for you."

From that day on, whenever I thought of us Belgians in the Congo, Mbulamatadis was what came to mind.

"Where does that come from, Mbulamatadis?" Mària asked.

"It's derived from Henry Morton Stanley's fondness for dynamite to blast through the Ngoma Mountain in the south."

"That's not very flattering," I said. "I don't care to be identified with Stanley."

"Me neither," Mària said.

"Stanley was very proud of Mbulamatadi." Father Brabant said. "It's on his tombstone."

"From what I've read of him, that fits," Mària said. "What do the Bantus call us to our face?"

"The Bantus call us Les Nokos, to our face. Uncle. Noko means uncle."

Father Brabant noted our bewilderment and tried to make light of the discordant pictures we were registering.

"Dissatisfied customers, are you?" he joked. He then became serious, out of concern, I suppose.

He may have aged but he had lost none of his urge to place things in a context only the power of his explanations could achieve.

"Like all Europeans," he announced, "you are experiencing your first-day-in-Africa letdown. As soon as you have become acclimated to the Congo, that will dissipate. Your minds will adjust, not because the Congo will have changed but because you will have bent to the opportunities to transform the place. And you'll thank God for these opportunities, and you'll become even more sympathetic toward the Congo; then you will turn into the champions of your captives. You see," he said at another point, "things are out of place in Leopoldville's Bantu sector; the people you're passing here belong in a forest or village somewhere out there; not in a city. What you're seeing is the pain of a village giving birth to a city. Such origins are always painful. I read that it was excruciating in Europe in the middle ages. In Africa, it's jarring."

But time didn't lessen the jarring of observing villagers learning to become city folks; time, instead, anesthetized me to the surroundings. To survive, I concentrated on the sick in my care, and I became an expert at treating people infected by the trypanosomiasis parasite that causes sleeping sickness. Seldom did I venture outside of my hospital. Certain events like the survival of Belgium's colonial effort preoccupied me significantly. However, after fifty-five years, I cannot say that I know the Congo. Mària, on the other hand, tried to survive by searching for a cause other than the ones Father Brabant had explained to us, a cause that would be reasonable to her, a cause she could assault.

The cause we wanted to assault immediately was our hunger. Mother Melchior had another idea. "Before going to the cafeteria," she told us, "It would be very wise for you to perform the *baciamano,* kiss the ring, of the Apostolic Vicar of Léopoldville[1], Bishop George Six. He is a congregant of the Immaculate Heart of Mary." That's where we went, of course.

Leaving behind the horror of Leopoldville's Bantu sector, we drove west to the government district of Kalina, which with Kinshasa comprised the European section of Leopoldville. The bishop and the governor general had their residences there.

When we approached the neutral zone between Leopoldville and Kalina, Father Brabant told us about the area we were about to drive though. "It's called the neutral zone," he explained, "a necessary buffer to protect the Belgian population from diseases emanating from the Bantu areas."

Mària moved her head slightly to the left to give me a questioning look. We learned that Mbulamatadis lived in

---

1.   http://www.catholic-hierarchy.org/diocese/dkins.html

terror of contamination. Labor needs being what they were, Mbulamatadis were not able to avoid the Bantus completely; so the colonial administration adopted a policy to make them as disease free as possible. Healthy natives would have fewer diseases to transmit to us Mbulamatadis. Several hospitals, dispensaries, laboratories, infirmaries, and other health facilities sprang up in the effort to make the African work force contagion free. Long past were the days of King Leopold II, who used African blood as fodder for his rubber plantations and had minimal concern towards health in his domain. (My uncle who was a member of the Belgian Workers Party loved to recount the trip he took in 1909 with his father to Laeken, a suburb of Brussels, for the express purpose of booing the funeral procession of Leopold II.)

The road into and the streets of Kalina were asphalted. The walled villas and houses painted all in white were overflowing with red and purple flowering bougainvilleas. The Bantus on the sidewalks were well dressed in khaki uniforms and colonial cork hats. Kalina must have been a well-fed district for there were garbage bins lining the route to our destination. Father Brabant had made no comment since telling us about the neutral zone. Perhaps he had seen Mària's head movement. The sway she had over him never failed to astound me.

With his white soutane and wide brown belt around the waist, Bishop Georges Six, Vicar Apostolic of Leopoldville was the classic colonial priest of the generation that felt duty-bound to impose the light of the church on the Bantus.

"I am from Vlamertinge," he told us, "a village in West Flanders."

Although Vlamertinge was less than forty kilometers north of Tournai, Bishop Six spoke French with a distinctive Flemish accent. He seemed pleased to see us, perhaps because of Mària, who had been unusually fervent in kissing his ring. I chatted with him as amiably as my nervousness and hunger permitted, while Mària stood to my right her eyes downcast, stone silent with apprehension, praying for both of us about what we had seen so far of our new home.

"Surely dear God, it wasn't meant to be that our first day would be the prologue and the finale to our journey here." She lifted her head once to follow the bishop's hand gesture. That was when he wanted to express the wide vista of the Congo, to tell us about upcountry stations and what to expect there. "For logistical reasons," he explained, "the bishopric decided that the missions would be primarily based in Leopoldville, to give better support to the upcountry stations."

Presently, Father Brabant, seeking to make light of our disappointing first impression of Leopoldville's Bantu sector was playing on our fondness for nature and everything pastoral. He didn't let a chance pass to extol what we had to look forward to upcountry. To hear him tell it, one would be forgiven to assume he was talking about the Swiss countryside. With all this talk of pastorals and bucolic paradise, we felt as if we were the sheep in the meadow between the rows of poplars at the Tournai diocese back home. It was not Easter, and we had not been fatted for slaughter; but we were starving. When the audience with the bishop finally concluded, we ran to the cafeteria downstairs, disregarding both good manners and sisterly demeanor, Father Brabant in the lead.

The Monday menu's fish and rice was bland. Father Brabant, who now seemed to have an excuse for everything, told us that was to accommodate the bishop's intolerance for spicy food. It didn't matter; hunger has a way of enhancing flavors, and we devoured the bland dish as if it were a gourmet steak and fries from Le Petit Chef, Tournai's finest restaurant. Eating the way we did eased Mother Melchior's concern about our state of mind. "I was worried about you," she told us. "I'm relieved that at least you still have a good appetite. That's a good sign." When she arrived at the cafeteria after us, we could tell that our running had annoyed her. She didn't scold us, probably because Father Brabant had run too. That she made Mària nervous was no surprise. Mària's aspiration was to set in motion Acts 4:35 of the gospel, *to each as any had need*. Mother Melchior on the other hand had for aspiration deference to the rules.

We welcomed the downpour that had started while we were in the cafeteria. It would screen the streets we had to pass through and we wouldn't have a graphic repeat of our earlier experience with the town.

Chapter 11

To recuperate from our travel and the other ordeals the Matadi to Leopoldville journey had inflicted on us, we could have, after our meal, opted that first day, to go to the two-bunk room reserved for us at the Sacred Heart Sisters' Residence in Kalina. However, we were too eager to go question the bureaucrats who ran the colony to try to rest in our room or mull over what we had seen of Leopoldville's Bantu sector. So we decided to go to the orientation and get acquainted services and put the formalities new-arrivals had to suffer through out of the way. The monsoon rain would screen the disagreeable scenes. The bureaucrats were in the administrative center contiguous to the bishopric, located in two buildings painted in lime paint of a yellowish color darkened by tropical mold spots. A vast garden of hibiscus bushes and travelers' palms with hundreds of native gardeners to tend them surrounded the buildings.

When we arrived in the Congo in October 1945, Pierre Ryckmans was still the Governor General. He was quite famous for having ignored King Leopold III's 1940 order to deny the allies access to the colonial forces under his command. My personal reason for wanting to wrap up the arrival formalities was Jerome, who had remained on my mind. I wanted to make inquiries regarding hiring him as a house servant. I spoke to Father Brabant about him at the cafeteria, and he promised to help. Not surprisingly, Mària was not interested in house servants. She did not say it, but the look she gave me when I mentioned house servant to Father Brabant was one of disapproval. Had Jerome already been judged a colonial *évolué*, a superior native, one who had adopted European values and mannerisms, the process of giving him a job would have been effortless. If only I had known, I could have simply stated, "Yes, he is an évolué," and that would have sufficed. As it happened, I had to slightly alter his biography to persuade the Congolese clerk who was assisting me at the administrative center that Jerome was similar to him, truly an évolué.

(I would find to my never-ending frustration that *évolués* like this clerk whose job it was to get us house servants were very protective of their status. They were as stingy as Moliere's miser regarding which and how many of their countrymen they would let in the club. I even detected an offended tone in the clerk's voice. Had it been anyone but Jerome, I would have let the clerk, who looked Jerome's age, designate a house servant for me. I did not budge, however. It had to be Jerome; and when Father Brabant, who was fervently trying to make up for our disappointment regarding Leopoldville's Bantu sector, intervened, the clerk found a reserve of alacrity and filled out the required form with Jerome's name on it. But it was up to me to bring Jerome from Matadi on the coast to Leopoldville. Father Brabant guessed what I was thinking, when I kept my eyes on the form as if it were a treasure map, and offered to take care of the matter the next day. This triumph took a load of my mind. Mària on the other hand had said very little since kissing the bishop's ring. She remained as she had since setting foot on Congolese soil – anxious. If there was a change, it was in the particular attention she paid to what the *évolués* we met at the bishopric and at the administrative center were telling us.

A successful colony is one that's run by the natives. Inside the administrative center buildings, *évolués,* sitting under ceiling fans, manned the information and permit booths. Arranged concentrically to maximize space, the booths were aligned in such a way as to remind new arrivals of the Stations of the Cross. To me it was just a labyrinth with pit stops.

When I noticed Mària's behavior and understood her mood, I prodded every *évolués* we met along the labyrinth to tell us what life was like upcountry. My love for her instructed me to try to make her look outward to a place poles apart from what we had seen, a place beyond the horror that the entire Congo might be like Leopoldville. I rose to the occasion, and for a short while, I moved out of Mària's shadow to give her hope. Unwittingly I benefited from the chance to upset the fate that I should live forever in that shadow; for soon, I would be alone, without Mària to block the sunlight of what the Congo had in store for me. The *évolués* cooperated wonderfully. They made photographs of the Congo's hinterland look like Switzerland's holiday posters. They had evidently experienced the way Europeans looked on Leopoldville's Bantu sector, and, ashamed or embarrassed, they sought to make us look instead on the interior of the Congo. The interior was still unspoiled by Europeans. African, the interior was idyllically pastoral and blissful; the people were as happy as the Swiss. It was what Rousseau had in mind in his essay about the sanctity of nature. Regardless of their motive, the *évolués* made us more impatient to leave Léopoldville to[1] its maladjustment; and neurotically we embraced the expectation that a transfer to an upcountry station would immunize us from what we had experienced

---

1.　　http://www.catholic-hierarchy.org/diocese/dkins.html

upon seeing life unfold in the streets of Léopoldville[2], a village in the throes of morphing into a city.

Like drowning travelers, we lashed onto the hope that upcountry was where we would find what we had come for in the Congo. Mària's earlier adherence to that German youth movement that favored countryside over city had something to do with the way we felt. Or perhaps it was the overwhelming apprehension that was choking us and driving us to give in to the conviction that the grass was greener wherever we were not. I held my tongue; Mària's disappointment didn't need any additional "I told you so" from me. We were in the Congo now, and nothing could turn that fact into a dream we would awaken from. But since it's a privilege of the old to blame youth for one's mistakes or misplaced feelings, I'll cash in that option now to remind myself that we were, if not spoiled, certainly immature young women, who happened to be nuns. Well-read, we certainly were; insightful, we were not. We sinned by our lack of other perspectives, any perspective that might have guided us through our feelings at the sight of our new home. We knew about transition anxiety in the abstract only, and I regret not having had back then a more solid understanding of what that anxiety was. Perhaps I would not have let it become the trauma that it did. How much that would've helped Mària, only the Trinity knows. Having reached the age when truthfulness is no longer a burden, I'll affirm that it's a myth that the young know no fear. The fact back then is that we were stricken by the kind of fear we felt was going to destroy us. And there was no buoy to help us from going under, not even fervent prayer.

2.	http://www.catholic-hierarchy.org/diocese/dkins.html

So with no other option but prayer, we put everything on imploring the almighty for an assignment to an upcountry station. That night in our room, even before Mària reached out for me, we intoxicated ourselves with the prospect of moving upcountry, desperate to be rescued from the anguish of having landed in Leopoldville. Mària found her voice during the night, and she expounded on how people *in nature* were a clean slate – she kept saying it in Latin, *tabula rasa* – and, therefore, receptive to new knowledge. In the interior of the Congo lived the adaptable Congolese; unlike the alienated ones we saw this morning. Upcountry was where opportunities awaited us like Gabon's Albert Schweitzer. Later in the night, I made a mental note to tell anyone who asked about screaming in the room that I had nightmares, a common occurrence upon landing in Leopoldville. Mària went bananas during her back-to-back fireworks, and she kept on turning her head like a whirlwind, making it impossible for me to put a lid on her scream at the octopus.

Mother Melchior did not disappoint us. She arrived at the cafeteria at breakfast with cheerful steps, a smile, and a secret. She couldn't wait to tell us in confidence that "It seems the bishop has taken a liking to you and is considering transferring you to an upcountry station as soon as transportation can be arranged."

It was now in our journey that the Congo turned into a tragic adventure. We stared at Mother Melchior, our eyes imploring her to tell us what the bishop was considering.

She smiled the smile renunciants reserve for good news. "Sister Mària would go as head mistress to the Kolwezi Orphanage for African Boys in the south," she said. Mària murmured, "Thank you Reverend Mother."

"It's a new orphanage we are building there," Mother Melchior continued, nudged on by Mària's words of gratitude, "to service not only southern Congo but also northern Angola and Zambia. Kolwezi is a strategic location for us. The end of the war has aggravated our competition with the Portuguese and the British for Africa and we must take steps to remain relevant."

Mària, a perfect renunciant, nodded another humble thanks; her face, however, was flushed with anticipation. I nodded too, expecting Mother Melchior to tell us that I would be going to Kolwezi as well. Perhaps as head nurse. Not once had it occurred to us that they would separate us; send us to different missions. Mother Melchior focused her stern eyes on me, and I gave her a sisterly smile of thanks.

"Sister Immanuel, you would go to Wembo-Nyama, in central Congo, to run the hospital there," she said to my dumbfounded eyes. After a pause to express bafflement that I had not responded the way Mària had, she continued, "Wembo-Nyama is also strategically located. As threatening as the European powers are to us, no threat is greater than the Anglo-Saxon's Evangelicals. Never forget that. The Methodists of one thing or another have been sniffing around Wembo since 1914. The hospital is what's keeping us pertinent."

I looked sideways at Mària. Her head was bowed in expectation; not in horror. I'm the one who was horrified. Susceptible to stress, I tended to be impulsive. I should have remained silent to get a broader picture of what the bishopric had in store for us, but unable to bear the strain Mother Melchior's announcement had caused me, I blurted out, "The Tournai diocese told us we would remain together." I didn't say more then, fearing that I would break down in sobs. Mària still kept her head lowered and remained silent. Love, in this case, did not dictate its laws. Mària had accepted our being split up, it seems. When it hit me that she had done that, I thought that my next breath would be my last. Repugnance and a modicum of uncertainty helped me control myself. I added softly with a hint of a nervous chuckle, "Does Father Brabant know about this? He promised us – ."

Mother Melchior looked at us in silence for a long time, as if she had made a great discovery about us, a mixture of apprehension and disapproval knotted her brow. Mària kept her head bowed. I kept my eyes on Mother Melchior. Then she focused only on me,

"Have you fallen in love, my child?" she asked, as if falling in love with Mària was as preordained as death. Angry, I almost asked her, have you? It was as close as I ever came to doing something I didn't do . . . and of attending a public hanging.

After our lustful episode at the bus-stop overhang in Tournai, we had flipped a coin, and I had won. If we were ever caught, I was the one who would do the denying first. I always thought that frightened would be my feeling, if that ever happened. At that moment, however, I had too much need for Mària to love me, and so much distress when she denied me that I couldn't be frightened. For that matter, I was too distraught to deny or say anything. My eyes were now on the tiny breakfast table around which the three of us were squeezed. I looked at it for a long while, and it became the symbol of how insignificant my life was in relation to having followed Mària to the Congo. Love is not about worshipping someone. Love is about being with someone. In my anguish, I had one proud moment of revelation. I actually whispered, "Thy will be done." Then I recited psalm 130. I had become a renunciant, a self-abnegating nun, my analects's most memorable moment.

Before I could reply to Mother Melchior's question, Mària gave a three dimensional answer, grimacing and shaking her head from side to side. Peter wasn't as emphatic in his denial of Christ. So much for unshakeable commitment! Mother Melchior keen to diffuse the explosiveness of the moment accepted Mària's denial and hurried to say, "Fine then. The bishop will no doubt consult Father Brabant. Where your service best serves the church will be their guide. How can it be otherwise? We all have to do our part to uphold the church that's being buffeted from all sides as a result of the war. Sacrifice, prayers and more sacrifice are needed –"

She said more about doing what was best for the church. I could not pay attention. Clichés couldn't give me relief from the absurd simplicity that my love had bumped into Mària's vocation. Taking the light of civilization to the darkness of *the least of these* was what I was up against. Then, too, I was too overwhelmed by my disillusion to hear someone remind me why I had come to the Congo. All I could think of was to get to Father Brabant. The Father Brabant, who mentored us in Tournai, could not live with himself without doing something to prevent sending Mària and me to different regions.

I knew what Mària was thinking, and it was not getting to Father Brabant to try to change our fate. She was trying to figure out how she was going to face me alone. She would do anything to delay the inevitable. She asked Mother Melchior, "What do you mean buffeted from all sides, Reverend Mother?" I looked up at the ceiling, praying that I would not explode.

Mother Melchior was too glad to expound on a matter of existential importance to the church. That she was oblivious to Mària's delaying tactic did not make it any more bearable for me.

"The war has turned the world upside down," Mother Melchior said in a tone she made disheartening. "Outside players are putting ideas in the heads of our natives."

"Outside players?" Mària asked innocently. Her voice was calm. She would not return my stare.

"The communists," Mother Melchior said as if it were an expletive.

For fifty-five years, I have thanked the Trinity everyday that I did not blurt out, "Here's your communist," pointing at Mària, as I ached to do. Remembering the devil's urge to say that about her, only Christ could have prevented it. He reached out at that instant and lifted the curse from me that we're the cause of our tragedies. Then, too, my engine was love; not revenge. I was spared taking revenge.

"That's spreading," Mother Melchior added. "Communism is spreading."

"I read that the French bring to Africa natives from their Caribbean colonies as administrators," Mària said. "A successful colony is one that's run by the natives." (She used my words.) "Why don't we do the same here? We can expand the pool of *évolués* like the ones we met with yesterday or bring them from Ruanda-Urundi. I understand we favor the Tutsis."

"Yes, we do," Mother Melchior said. They're our most handsome natives. I just love the Tutsis. They remind me of the most graceful giraffes. Why don't you mention the Tutsis to the bishop when you see him? He approves of you. He could order that your Kolwezi orphanage start a program to create a cadre of Tutsi proxies to help in administration. I would certainly support that."

I couldn't take it anymore – Mària hoodwinking Mother Melchior like that. I touched my chest and with all the deference I could muster, I interjected, "Reverend Mother, Father Brabant asked us to meet him this morning at the administrative center to finalize some paperwork. May I be excused?"

That was true; Father Brabant had asked me to join him at the administrative center to complete the formalities that would permit a native, my Jerome, to travel from Matadi to Leopoldville.

"Yes, my child, of course," Mother Melchior said. My distrustful heart did not fail to wonder if she wasn't glad to be rid of me. I looked in Mària's direction, expecting that she would follow me. That she would be eager to go with me to appeal to Father Brabant, who, back in Tournai, had not been able to refuse her anything.

"I'm very interested in Sister Mària's understanding of the administration of the colonies," Mother Melchior said. "She'll join you shortly."

I turned, bowed to Mother Melchior and walked out of the cafeteria. The Sainte Thérèse de la Sainte-Face,The Saint Therese of the Holy Face chapel was across from the cafeteria's entrance, but I did not go in to implore Sainte Thérèse, who was the saint under whose benefaction I completed my novitiate, to infuse Father Brabant with all the zeal in the world to get Mària and me a common assignment.

Chapter 12

To be alone for a while, I went up to our room at the Sacred Heart Sisters' Residence where Mària and I had spent the night. A house cleaner was there. In a fatigued voice I remember well, I told her to come back later, and I sat on the bed where love had been exulted during the night. She left, closing the door softly behind her, a certain smile on her face. More than half a century later, I still wonder if that smile wasn't for what was left of our frolic in that room, the tang that lingered. I felt the soreness in the frenulum of my tongue and that inevitably brought to mind the woodcut, *The Dream of the Fisherman's Wife*. Until today, I think that was the last time I thought of that wonderful octopus, executing an inspired cunnilingus for the fisherman's wife. I never cried; but wondering how Mària was going to cope, I became so disconcerted I burst into tears. We women make love for love. That's why we are not afraid of our desires, any more than our feelings. Whether or not Mària found a lover, I knew that our kind of lovemaking, the kind you lose consciousness in one another, would be over. It was not just anguish expressing itself. I opened the nightstand's drawer and pulled out the bottle of local brandy made of cassava roots that the evening's house cleaner had gotten for me. That and Kisikisi, a brew made of wild sorghum, were to be my staple liquors while in the Congo.

Before going to meet Father Brabant, I brushed my teeth, gargled thoroughly, and changed into the second habit the diocese had issued to us upon our arrival, the day before. I stood at the closet and lifted the sleeve of the one Mària had worn during our travel from Matadi to Leopoldville and sniffed as deeply as my unhappiness permitted me to do.

I loved the all-white habit we wore in the tropics. Pure as if anointed by the faith, it was not only more comfortable against the heat, it was also so much more distinctive than the others. I was very proud of it for that; not because the natives were in superstitious awe of it due to their association between the color white and the ghost of their ancestors. Then, too, it made me look like Mària. Breaking the rules, for fifty years I had a green piece of rope to hang a crucifix that I wore at the waist on Fridays. That way I could be like her the Friday I first saw her in Miss Gerard's class back in '34. I knew it would be a challenge keeping it spotless, but I promised myself that I would change as often as necessary to maintain an immaculate appearance. Jerome, without telling him, took on the challenge. Soon after his arrival, he went to the Leopoldville central market, where he found the tailor, who specialized in duplicating garments for expats. There were always two laundered and starched habits hanging in the closet for me to wear.

I did not want to keep Father Brabant waiting. I also did not want to appeal to him without considering first what I should say. On the way out, I peeked inside the cafeteria. Mària was still in there hoodwinking poor Mother Melchior.

To keep debilitating stress at bay, I tried to examine what had come my way as thoroughly as possible. I still try to reduce the intense discomfort stress causes me, although it's meaningless now; and brandy not only works faster but provides for my other needs as well. It is, however, one thing to be aware of one's nature and try to adjust; it is another to squash or even modulate it. That morning, I got ready by memorizing what I was going to say to Father Brabant. I took a rosary-prayer stroll among the hibiscus bushes and the traveler palms in the garden surrounding the buildings during a lull in the monsoon rain. Thirty minutes passed quickly. I walked to the colonial administration building. Father Brabant, punctual as ever, his shoulders caved in, was already there ambling from one column to another on the veranda of the administration building's entrance, his hands behind his back. My heart sank more when I noticed that he looked deep in thought. He is deep in figuring out how he's going to tell me that Mària and I are going to different regions, I told myself.

Although accusatory, my words as planned were doused in a pleading tone. "How could you've given the go ahead for Mària and me to go to different places?" I said, shaking my head, my eyes downcast, when I got close to him. I had practice using pleading tones since entering my aunt's house in 1934; I was well practiced to it.

You couldn't talk to many priests that way back then, no matter how long you'd known them. Most of them practiced various forms and degrees of severity as if they were cassock requirements. Father Brabant was different. To Mària and me, who had grown up in his shadow, he was like a parent. I could be familiar with him regarding personal matters.

"Sister Melchior told you?" he said.

"Yes."

"She moved fast."

"What do you mean?"

"She's suspicious of you. Thinks the two of you are too close . . . used the word unhealthful. That's what she told the bishop. They've been together a long time. Her influence in that office is considerable."

"Well," I said, "you're the reason we're here. You're not –"

"I will do all I can to prevent it from happening," he interjected. "I'll tell you here what I told you in Tournai, the church is better served with you together."

"You don't sound as if the bishop is going to listen to you," I said. My negative appraisal contrasted with his positive tone.

"Sister Melchior's influence over the bishop is strong," he said. "And she wants you in separate regions."

"What are you going to do then?" I said.

"I will try to persuade him that you are an effective team. Together you provide much more to the church than apart. He's a reasonable superior; he'll give me a hearing. If that fails and you're separated, it will not be for long. The bishop must retire soon. As auxiliary I'm his assigned successor. Once the miter is placed on my head, I will send you to where Sister Mària is or vice versa. By the time the Baobab outside your window is in bloom, you'll be together."

"Two years. I don't know what we'll do."

"If that comes to pass, you'll write each other long coded letters. You will also have your work. You'll be too tired to reflect on your personal woes. Think of this as a sacrifice, an offering to the Almighty. Nothing is done, however, until the bishop signs the order."

"I'm afraid for Mària," I said as much to help me recover from the father's remark about coded letters as to express my fear for Mària. "That depression back in Tournai, that was just a few months ago. You should not dismiss that lightly. She is as fragile as glass. If you cannot keep us together, you should send her back to the motherhouse in Liege."

Father Brabant's five-year tropical suntan became multiple shades paler. "Are you serious?" he said.

"Oh very," I said. "She is as brittle as a wafer."

"I'll have to tell the bishop then. Let's hurry to complete the business of your house servant, and I'll go see the bishop before he leaves for his tour of our northern missions."

We went in the administration building and walked side by side to the desk of the *évolué* responsible for getting house servants for new arrivals. He stood up when he saw us approaching, took a form from the top of his desk and waved it as if eager to show he was on top of things or perhaps he was just eager to make amends for his lack of alacrity the day before.

"Father, Sister," he said. "It is all arranged. Mr. Jerome has his official permit to travel to Leopoldville." Father Brabant patted his head.

I said, "Thank you my son;" took the paper from his hand and handed it over to Father Brabant. He turned to leave. I nodded to the *évolué* and followed.

On the veranda, Father Brabant stopped a couple of meters away from the entrance to the àdministration building and faced me.

"I have an idea," he said. "A demonstration of what I mean by what an effective team you and Sister Mària make."

I looked at him both eagerly and suspiciously.

"While you're staying in Kalina," he continued, "you can do morning or night shifts at the Queen Elisabeth Clinic with Sister Mària as your assistant. It's around the corner from your quarters. That will take your situation off your minds and show the bishop what I mean by together you provide more to the church than apart."

"Very well, Father," I said. Anything that would keep Mària and me together was fine with me. "Yes." Suspicion had vanished.

"I'll go to the bishop now," he said. "He lives in dread of tsetse flies and contagion, he'll probably dither as he always does, and I'll be able to catch him.

"I'll tell Mother Melchior about your lending a hand at the Queen Elisabeth Clinic," he added. "It's the perfect facility for an introduction to the practice of medicine in the Congo." He opened his umbrella and walked off, leaving me on the veranda. He had taken two steps in the rain when he remembered something and came back. "Watch out for the servants at the Sacred Heart Sisters' Residence," he said. "They report to Mother Melchior."

Chapter 13

The Queen Elisabeth Clinic was a splendidly simple all white art deco complex, consisting of eleven buildings built fifteen years earlier, a blast from the past. The chief architect at the Colonial Public Works Department, Richard Lequy, was the mastermind behind it. I got to meet him while staying at the Sacred Heart Sisters' Residence in Kalina. In 1945, the clinic had beds for Europeans only, 202 for men and 58 for women and children.

I had two choices, go to the room at the Sacred Heart Sisters' Residence to wait for Mària, or I could go visit the clinic. I chose to go to the clinic because I desperately wanted to have Mària in my arms and commiserate with her on our fate; but I knew I wouldn't be able to do that, given the anger underneath my feeling. A visit to the clinic would give me time to equalize my conflicted states of mind.

The clinic wasn't far; I could see it from the administration building's veranda. I opened my umbrella and stepped out in the rain that had resumed but was still taking a respite from the downpour of the early morning. I continued my rosary at the eleventh decade, where I had left off earlier and crossed the part of the garden closest to the chapel attached to the complex's main building.

Often, I have thought of the Queen Elisabeth Clinic's Sainte Anne chapel. It represented Belgium's colonial mindset. Also designed in the art deco style by Richard Lequy, it complemented perfectly the clinic's simple architecture. Inside was a vibrant and modern place of worship. The panoply of organ pipes looked shiny new. And the sanctuary and the nave had the feel of one of our smaller Belgian cathedrals with the exception that it was awash in light. If the colonial administration could build such a house of worship in Kalina, why couldn't they do the same in the rest of Leopoldville, to impress the natives with a show of equality, for instance? Later I was able to ask Richard Lequy why he hadn't designed churches like the clinic's chapel for the Bantus?

"I wouldn't mind," he said. "But the governor was adamantly opposed to equivalencies between European and Bantu. He maintained that, 'Such designs would be wasted on the natives; they would not appreciate them,' and 'They may get the notion they are no different from Belgians.'"

I knelt at the altar. As always, I began my prayer with the act of contrition, *Deus meus, ex toto corde poenitet me omnium meorum peccatorum* ... and as always found succor in asking for pardon. I then completed the rosary. Feeling the tiny spiritual part of me refreshed, my eyes moist, I left the misplaced chapel, looking forward to coming back while in Kalina.

Next door was the clinic's main building. I went up its steps and entered a well-lighted white hall, to be welcomed at the information desk by an older Flemish woman dressed in her Sunday best. She was the wife of a colonial official. "A volunteer at the clinic," she told me giddily. She confessed that she and her husband had expatriated themselves to the Congo because in Belgium they were accusing the Flemish community of collaboration with the Germans. I listened patiently. Something happened back then when I introduced myself to people: I put on a veil of modesty beyond the low-key manner expected of a nun. I was a sinner, you see, and it befitted my awareness to be modest. I seemed to be reasoning that if I am appropriately modest, my sin will not be noticeable. It was not the same with Mària. Whether or not she wished to appear unassuming, she was too striking to be successful. She was left to watch others be unassuming towards her. Such was the role of appearance in our lives back then. Fortunately or not, in a few years, I grew out of the feeling I had to be self-effacing. Instead, I grew into an arrogant and invariably austere nun. Millions of acts of contrition helped me modulate arrogance. However, after thirty years, I gave up trying to appear less austere.

The volunteer gave me directions to the nurses' station on the second floor. There I recognized a Missionary Franciscan Sister of Marie whose name I remembered then but have since forgotten. She had been at the Institute of Tropical medicine at Antwerp when I was studying there. I remember addressing her by her name, and she gave me a second, longer look before recalling the institute and me. My white habit had changed the way I looked, she said. Humility obliging, she told me that she had not been able to complete the institute's curriculum and had been assigned as an orderly at the Queen Elisabeth Clinic while she tried for a correspondence certificate. She had already been in Kalina a bit over a year and liked it there.

We chatted for a while, until the assistant administrator, Mother Sainte-Ursule, arrived. My classmate introduced me by way of singing my praise for what she called my reputation at the institute. I perceived that she was embarrassed for having fallen short at Antwerp, and I told her when we were alone a while that I would help her with her correspondence coursework. In front of me, Mother Sainte-Ursule broke the convent's no-touching rule, to pat her sympathetically on the sleeve. That impressed me immensely, and I eagerly told Mother Sainte-Ursule why I had come to the clinic.

"A graduate of the institute is very valuable here," she told me weighting her words carefully, when we were alone in her office. Then came the disapproval, "Had you been with the Missionary Franciscan Sisters of Marie, you would have been in time a full fledge physician. I am a generalist; Mother Hélène, our administrator, is a gastroenterologist. The authority is with us physicians. We are not second class anything here." She said the last part with clenched teeth.

What in the world I asked myself taken aback by the vehemence I didn't see coming. The criticism had stung, however, and I said, "The time it took to complete the medical curriculum was overly long."

Mother Sainte-Ursule stated her disagreement with a shake of the head. "I will tell Doctor Hélène to expect you," she said; then on second thought she added (how can I forget) "Doctor Hélène is with a dysentery patient. If you've the time, let's walk next door and I'll introduce you."

Mother or doctor Hélène of the Missionary Franciscan Sisters of Marie, head of the Queen Elisabeth Clinic in Kalina, was a middle aged woman on the petite side. She was coming out of an examination room when Mother Sainte-Ursule spotted her and called out, "Doctor Hélène, there is a sister freshly graduated from the institute I want you to meet." When I got close to her, I detected powder on her face. I was sure of it, and so surprised was I, my face felt as if it had been pressed against a lighted stove. She extended two fingers from her left hand and Mother Sainte-Ursule retrieve a pack of cigarettes from her pocket and extended it to her. She took one and lighted it herself with an engraved Cartier gold lighter. She was the most confident woman I had ever met. Her movements were quick, assured; and even before Mother Sainte-Ursule introduced me, she had already given me a quick look and made up her mind about me.

"You're not of the Missionary Franciscan Sisters," she said in what I took for a disappointed voice.

"No Reverend Mother," I said, "the Perpetual Cross is my order."

"A communist must have thought of creating an order to serve the least of these." she said lightly as if apologizing for stating a widely-held view. At that, Mother Sainte-Ursule stepped in to introduce me, repeating the words the other Franciscan Sister had lauded me with. She then explained why I was at the Queen Elisabeth Clinic.

"Fine," Mother/Doctor Hélène said. "We have a gastroenteritis patient who needs looking after. I'm counting that you're familiar with the gastroenteritis syllabus that I wrote for them at Antwerp. When you and Sister Sainte Marie report to Doctor Ursule, you'll be assigned to that patient. He's a hopeless French economist. He also thinks in term of the least of these. You should get along fine." With that, she took a drag on her cigarette and abruptly turned and continued on her way.

She left me wondering by what magic she had connected *the least of these* with the communists. Was everyone in authority in the colony obsessed with communists? It didn't take me long to figure out that the Bantus' strong opposition to colonialism was used as an excuse to brand them as communists.

Mother Sainte-Ursule and I went back to the nurses' station the way we came, chatting about why we were in the Congo. "Doctor Hélène likes you," she said, when I opened the door for her. "She doesn't joke with just anybody. I hope you know that what she said about the Perpetual Cross was an attempt at humor."

"I'm not offended, Reverend Mother, if that's what's concerning you," I said with as much of a hint of a smile as I could manage.

"Yes, but Doctor Hélène and Mother Melchior do not get along. Not at all," she said. "And Melchior has authority with the bishop."

"You mean that Mother Melchior will counter Father Brabant's request? And the bishop will listen to her." What I was actually thinking was that Mother Melchior was going to separate me from Mària and there was not much Father Brabant could do about it.

"That's exactly what I'm saying," Mother Sainte-Ursule said. "I'm sure Doctor Hélène is presently calling the governor, who will call the bishop. That's why I wanted you to meet her right away."

"The governor," I said, probably sounding like the innocent girl in the forest.

"Yes," she insisted. "We are the physicians. In a place where the fear of catching something from the natives is as commanding as the fear of the plague in the fourteenth-century, it's the medicine man that has the last word."

Right away I thought, if that's the case, Doctor Hélène could contrive to have the governor intervene to keep Mària and me in Kalina as permanent members of her staff. And what's more, Mària – Sister Sainte Marie – would be thrilled to be in the company of iconoclasts like Doctors Hélène and Mother Sainte-Ursule. The fire in my loins was suddenly blazing again.

At the nurses'station she said, "Not to worry. . . there's nothing in the holy rules that says you cannot smile."

I thanked her and attempted a smile and left to go to Father Brabant's office at the bishopric, to see whether I should no longer worry and indeed have something to smile about. The bishopric was adjacent to the administrative center. Retracing my steps, I stopped for an Ave Mària at the chapel and upon retrospection another act of contrition. From the chapel, I crossed the garden nearest the administrative center. A troupe of absorbed monkeys in single file passed me without a second look. I then went in the building to thank the *évolué* once more for the permit he had granted Jerome to travel to Leopoldville. Waiting for me on the veranda was Father Brabant. He must have seen me from the bishopric's balcony walking through the garden while the rain was resting.

"It was a mistake to go to the clinic and speak to Mother Hélène," he said without preamble, a mixture of concern and irritation in his voice.

I looked at him, questioningly.

"Mother Hélène called the governor in your behalf, and he called the bishop, unnecessarily it turned out."

I put a look of concern on my face. As if holding my breath, I tried to keep the stress in. Stress from all the disappointments plus the bureaucratic rigmarole Mària and I had to put up with, having been in the Congo only two days.

"The bishop had already agreed to your internship at the clinic," Father Brabant said. "But he finds amusement in the scraps Mother Hélène engages in with Mother Melchior, and so he told her what Mother Hélène had done. Mother Melchior is not pleased. She was even curt with me, when I told her about you and the clinic."

I too was not pleased. What could Mother Melchior do against Mother Hélène, the doctor of medicine? She could, however, take her ill will on Mària and me. I was beginning to wonder if the Congo would not be our Via Dolorosa. After Mària surrendered her life, I thought that I would not have to think in terms of Calvary anymore. However, it took more than forty years for that notion to morph into something else.

"I just wanted to see what the clinic looked like," I said. Under the stress, my heart had hardened in the meantime; and I let go with a sharpened voice. "How can I be responsible for what goes on between two superiors here? I arrived yesterday, remember." I looked at the father, my head tilted questioningly to one side.

No one joins a religious order unless prepared to follow the rules, the first of which is obedience. For us, obedience is not just doing what one is told. Obedience is humility, and subservience to the will of one's order. Obedience is following one's superiors, and it is deference to the ancient instruments of authority. Had it been anyone else, I would have been reprimanded and punished for just stating the facts. I don't remember fifty-five years later, but I doubt that I would have stated the facts so pointedly to someone else. I certainly never did again. Father Brabant had from our beginning at the Tournai diocese, encouraged Mària and me to express ourselves. He did not seek to stamp out our individuality as he was supposed to.

He liked to say, "A beard doesn't make a philosopher," or "It's not the habit that makes the nun."

Ours was a unique association. As much as I was grateful for it then, I'm glad now there weren't more nuns and priests like us; for had there been more, the organization of the church would have suffered more afflictions than it has. Father Brabant permitted us to operate outside of the echo chamber of the traditional nun and priesthood. He gave us the flexibility that enabled Mària and me to rise above our position of subordinate and superior, priest and nun, but also of mentor and apprentice. He was as invested in us as he was in the Congo, and he sought to look after what he had produced.

That's my take on why he behaved toward us the way he did. Fifty-five years later, propped on Jerome's pillows in my suite in Maison St Jean's nursing home, I have not forgotten the meaning of our story, and I can look back in wonder on that event back in October 1945, standing on the veranda of the colony's administration building. Father Brabant was ahead of his time. While being the source of our Congolese adventure, he was also the source of our devotion to that rich but destitute land in the middle of Africa. The Congolese cherished him for his open-mindedness and his efforts to lessen the exploitative nature of the relationship between colonizer and colonized. There was no false pretense in him. He was maniacally opposed to holding the catechism in one hand and the colonial mandate in the other to make Belgian rule over the Congo as comprehensive as possible – until he became Bishop of Leopoldville and sought to burnish his colonial credentials by trying to alter the Congolese tradition of worship. For that, he too surrendered his life. I look on him today as the St. Sebastian of Belgium's colonial effort in Africa. Because he was someone I could go to when the simple desire to reveal the condition of my soul was upon me, I mourn him almost as much as I mourn Mària.

He said, "I learned a Congolese proverb I'd like to share with you, 'Only a naïve person tests the depth of a river with both feet.'"

"I get your point," I said, "and I will pay heed to its truth." We were back to having a conversation. Then I saw the troupe of monkeys in the back garden, and I asked pointing at them. "Do you know what monkeys these are?"

"They're called pygmy chimpanzees," he said. (They'd be called *bolobos* ten years later, after a village north of Leopoldville. Later on, *bonobos*.) "The natives believe, and I believe, they are the spirit of the administrative center's garden, here to keep an eye on us. They believe in love above everything else."

I excused myself before he started expounding on love, as was his wont. Turning around to leave, I repeated, "I get your point about the proverb." It was time to go find Mària, confident that she already knew about the clinic.

I had been thinking about a toy we had named "Black Octopus" because it was made out of black rubber. I was mulling over how I would shut my ears to her "enough" cries. It's strange to find out that there are no rules for achieving sexual goals, that lustful urges can turn into urges to hurt a loved one, and that the body can be just as unhappy as the mind.

I walked to the Sacred Heart Sisters' Residence. I remember thinking that a white umbrella was just what we needed to go with our white attire. Halfheartedly, I opened the black one I was carrying. The dampness had made my habit feel as if I had it on for days and not for a few hours, and I looked forward to changing it.

Mària couldn't still be in the residence's cafeteria, but I peeked in anyway. Only waiters where there, getting the place ready for lunch. At the bottom of the stairs to the room for visiting nuns, I looked up at the longest flight of stairs I was ever going to take. My entire life was playing out in front of me. Worse, I couldn't stop Mària from humming the overture to La Forza del Destino in my head. Camille, I even saw the entire film. After my life, Verdi, and Camille were done, I found my hope for me and Mària waiting in one of the rooms upstairs. I moved slowly, taking one step after another, until I was standing at the door where I was sure Mària was waiting. It was unlocked.

I turned the knob and walked in. Mària was in prayer, seating on the bunk against the far wall, near the window. As swift as a hummingbird she bolted up and ran to me. Her arms around my neck, she cried out,

"You've done it Octopus of mine. You've done it."

She then pressed her mouth against mine her tongue in the vanguard of a kiss. My mouth remained shut. I was deflated, my resentment towards her replaced by astonishment. She pulled away, too agitated to care. Had I not witnessed some of her moments of manic agitation before, I would have been afraid.

She wrung her hands, sweated and spoke nonstop about how we would remain together now that we had the clinic as a refuge. Soon she would be exhausted and sleep. She would awaken coherent and ready to face our reality. The Tournai diocese and the Perpetual Cross convent in liege had noticed that she could be 'moody;' but they were too overtaken by her look and charisma to say more than 'she can be a little eccentric at times.'

Maria's personality traits were meant to be erased by the Blessed Rules of the nuns, smoothing out any eccentricities or flaws she may have had. If that were true, Mària would have no connection to herself. She would embody a blank canvas in the narrative of rejecting nature. She would be devoid of any vitality, like a melted wax tablet.

Chapter 14

Mària was sleeping when Mother Melchior walked in. I was coming out of the bathroom. It was her prerogative not to knock, but until then, I had never experienced a Mother Superior doing that. The fear that she would take her spite about interning at the clinic on Mària and me was coming true sooner than I had imagined. My stress level soared, and I thrash around in my head for a way that would help me remain calm. Fortunately, she began speaking the instant she entered the room:

"Hélène is the devil incarnate," she said, as she was sitting down on one of the two chairs in the room. No preamble seemed necessary. "She's an Anti-Christ the bible warned us against." Her face flushed crimson with antipathy toward Doctor Hélène. Thank God I never experienced such ill feelings toward anyone.

"She assumes that being a medical doctor prevails against the holy community of nuns," she continued more matter-of-factly, as if she were now talking about the baobab tree outside the window. "It does not. A doctor of the soul is what a nun is first. A camel will go thru the eye of a needle before Hélène sees the Kingdom."

That conclusion spoken loudly woke Mària up.

"Did I scream?" a dazed Mària asked.

"No," I rushed to answer. Mària sat down demurely on her bunk and after a moment said,

"Reverend Mother, how good of you to visit us."

"I have a duty to protect you from evil," Mother Melchior replied."

"From the communists?" Mària asked. I would have sworn she was making fun of Mother Melchior.

"A false prophet in the guise of Sister Hélène," the superior answered.

"I don't know Sister Hélène," Mària said in her most diffident pose.

"You will when you go to that clinic. It's not just the communists we have to fear. It's also the Hélènes of the world, synonym for Mammon in the Infernal Dictionary. The Hélènes, who are corrupting the sisterhood. Nothing good can come of your experience at that clinic. Father Brabant notwithstanding, you should have gone to where I told you this morning without delay."

Mother Melchior then rose from the chair; walked to the nightstand by the window, and opened the drawer. My heart sank. It hit me like one of Mària's screams that the smiling housekeeper had told Mother Melchior about my local brandy. She then walked to the other nightstand and removed the half-full bottle.

"Spend all your free time in prayer – plead for patience," she then said. "And wear an apparel to remind you that patience is God's path. In your sight, there should be God and only God."

Without pausing even for breath, she added, "Sister Mària, I want you to play the organ in the chapel. The bishop is very fond of Bach's Toccata and Fugue in D minor. He likes it fortissimo. None of that insincere pianissimo, please."

"Fortissimo is how I play it," Mària said with the smile that dazzled. "Our bishop in Tournai did not like it and made me stop. I haven't played since."

"You'll have some practice while you're here, then," Mother Melchior said.

There was a bureau near the door. Mother Melchior placed the half-full bottle of local brandy on its top as if it were something precious. "If you must drink brandy," she said, I'll have a bottle of Monnet for you after you've reported what an evil creature Hélène is. Or absinth, which wards off malaria." On that, she opened the door and walked out, leaving Maria breathless.

I wanted to talk, expunge my stress and strategize our comportment in light of what we had learned since arriving in Leopoldville. Mària, however, wanted to go to the chapel to see the pipe organ. We agreed that we would talk while walking there. We would not enter the chapel until we were satisfied.

Chapter 15

While Mother Sainte-Ursule stood at my side smiling, Doctor Hélène, a cigarette between her lips, stared at Mària for half a minute. "I'm pleased to make your acquaintance my child," she said. "I would be remiss if I did not say that I wish with all my heart that you and Sister Immanuel were of the Missionary Franciscan Sisters."

"Thank you Reverend Mother," Mària said.

"I prefer Doctor Hélène."

I was shocked to hear Mària say, "If you insist."

Doctor Hélène saw my reaction. She lifted her head, looking distressed. "So, Saint Melchior has had a round about me with you," she said. "No doubt with her inimitable vocabulary. No doubt. I would be remiss if I did not say that you disappoint me. I thought you were . . . special. The vineyard needs progressive minds, my child, to take it into a self-determined future. Useful nuns, that's what the Congo needs; not colonialists in the guise of saints. Tsetse flies can be saints. Does this vineyard need more tsetse flies, my child?"

"No Doctor Hélène," Mària answered.

"I thought so. I couldn't be that wrong about someone." She smiled in the direction of Mother Sainte-Ursule.

"Yves Aubert is a French economist with a degree from Harvard University in the United States of America," Mother Sainte-Ursule explained. "He arrived here on his own dime two months ago, lured by the mythology of the Congo, heart of darkness, noble savage, big-bottom women, that sort of nonsense. He met the governor, who hired him as a consultant. He's taken up with the Italian exotic dancer at the officers' club." She paused to light a cigarette and take a long pull from what Mària called "Those awful things." When she was quenched, she continued, "The dancer is the one who brought him to us. Doctor Hélène diagnosed severe protozoan dysentery and is keeping him under observation. He seems anxious, complained of hearing noises; something dysentery would not cause. He's a pleasant fellow enough, when not erratic. Apologizes every few minutes, but refuses to take his quinine. He swears by cannabis, which grows readily here. Your job is to watch over him. Make sure he takes his metronidazole and nalidixit. Sister Mària, I'll take you to his room. You'll have the first watch."

Mària was pleased. She nodded to me with a "We're on our way" wink and went with Mother Sainte-Ursule.

Twenty minutes later, she walked in the nurses' station. Mother Sainte-Ursule and I were discussing a job description for her; also the fact that there would be different phases in our absorption into the clinic's staff structure. Meanwhile, Doctor Hélène would do all in her power to keep us in place. My sense about the clinic director was that she would not take no for an answer, and that Mària and I would ensconce ourselves in Kalina. That being the case, I got ahead of myself, being sure that Doctor Hélène would be enthralled by Mària's mind and give her a job in the clinic's administration department. I had just told Mother Sainte-Ursule to arrange for them to spend time together, when Mària walked in. She was pale but not panicky. If it had been me, I would've been both pale and panicky.

"I've lost my patient," she said. "I was telling him about his medication, when he said he had to go to the bathroom. I waited for him to come back. After ten minutes, I went to the bathroom and knocked. There was no answer. The door was opened. He was not there.

We started to search for Yves Aubert. Eventually Mother Sainte-Ursule reached the first floor. At the information desk, another Flemish volunteer said when asked, "To think of it, Mother Sainte-Ursule, a man who appeared to be dressed in hospital garbs hurriedly walked out twenty minutes ago."

By then Yves Aubert was dead. When Mother Sainte-Ursule and I stepped outside, we noticed a crowd of Africans that was surrounding his body on the ground, in front of the chapel. From their telling of what they saw, it was a straightforward affair. Aubert left the bathroom and ran down the four flights of stairs to the first floor. He walked out of the clinic and ran to the Sainte Anne Chapel. He ran up twelve flights of stairs to the belfry of the chapel, the tallest building in Kalina at that time. The Congolese screaming that he was going to get killed, he hoisted himself to the roof of the belfry and without pausing a second he threw his body headfirst over the side, falling on the Swiss Consul General's car parked outside of the chapel. He bounced off onto the pavement in front of the chapel.

Behind us, I saw Mària on the steps of the clinic, her eyes wide, piercing red blotch of distress on each cheek. We never touched in public. We followed the rules. Here, I went to her as close as I dared to whisper, "This is one man who had the devil on his heels." She turned her head to give me a look replete with grief. And as if remembering, she said, "The Russians have landed," our code for when we were menstruating. If that were the only effect this had on her, I thought, that wasn't bad. I almost laughed. Doctor Hélène appeared, her face contorted with shock and rage.

"What happened here?" she asked in an infuriated yet brittle voice. "I've never lost a patient this way."

Little did I know that her humanity, her humility, her spirituality all revolved around that statement?

Everything that happened next was to be determined by Doctor Hélène's "I've never lost a patient this way," a blight she considered was on her record now. Resentment like stormy clouds darkened her view of Mària and me and drove how she dealt with us. Gone was any notion that she would make an effort to integrate us into her staff at the clinic. I sensed it the moment she spoke, like a foreshadowing of what was to come.

After the tragedy had had its way with us, we learned from the coroner who learned from the officers' club dancer that Yves Aubert was taking chlorpromazine that he had brought with him from France. Chlorpromazine was then a new drug prescribed for the treatment of schizophrenia. She told the coroner that she had made him take cannabis instead.

"I don't believe in pills. I use cannabis for everything," she told the coroner.

Sister Sainte-Dominique, the mental health nurse practitioner at the clinic, also a Missionary Franciscan Sister, explained to the coroner that withdrawal from the schizophrenia medication, combined with the medications for the protozoan dysentery he was prescribed, threw Aubert into a suicidal tailspin, and he became desperate to kill himself. Nevertheless, Doctor Hélène did not consider that diagnosis sufficient to remove the stain that was now smearing her record, still maintaining that Mària and I had had a role in inflicting that stain on her.

Nothing could be more unfair. Doctor Hélène was responsible not only for her lack of due diligence in prescribing metronidazole and nalidixit in light of what was learned about Yves Aubert's condition but also for being lackadaisical in assigning Mària to monitor a patient who should have been on suicide watch. The last criticism stuck, and Doctor Hélène blamed Mother Sainte-Ursule. As to her prescribing metronidazole and nalidixit, she argued that only a medical board of inquiry could second-guess her. Doctor Hélène was guilty. Mària responded with feelings of intense hostility, made worse by having to suppress them according to convent rules. Nonetheless, those feelings toward the superior made the sorrow she felt for the suicide of Yves Aubert less difficult to bear. She held up well. Mother Melchior was, of course, there to fan that hostility, telling Mària what an immature, selfish, and vain fiend Doctor Hélène was, words Mària wanted to hear to feed her outrage. No doubt Mother Melchior disparaged the doctor at the bishopric, where she had unrestricted access. Soon the rumor that the bishop had found Doctor Hélène negligent was loud enough for everyone in Kalina to be aware of it. However, the Missionary Franciscan Sisters worked for the Belgian government that had hired the congregation to staff the Queen Elisabeth Clinic. As such, Governor Pierre Ryckmans had the final decision as to whether or not Doctor Hélène maintained her position at the clinic. Parties pro and con formed to support or denounce her. Then to my consternation, Mària would have nothing to do with the Queen Elisabeth Clinic as long as Doctor Hélène was in charge. She spent most of her time with Mother Melchior, who found "Her accessible mind most delightful." I continued to go although they mistrusted me there. I went because I was hoping for a change of heart. Doctor Hélène ignored me, and I dealt solely with Mother Sainte-Ursule, who was sympathetic.

"This man was out to suicide," she would say. "Only God could have prevented him. He chose not to. And he killed himself."

They gave me night shifts, and I saw patients on a limited basis. Having been demoted, there was nothing of substance for me to do; I was, as they say, all dressed up with nowhere to go, and unless there was a change of director or of heart, my days at that clinic would be a purgatory.

At a meeting with Father Brabant the morning of our third day in the Congo, I related to him what Mother Sainte-Ursule had said about the preeminence of physicians where the fear of catching a disease from the natives was an obsession. Father Brabant agreed that was true and would have started a lecture had Mària not interrupted him to announce that she would follow his suggestion and mine and confess carelessness in the suicide of Yves Aubert and beg Doctor Hélène to keep us at the clinic. He made the appointment for the three of us later that morning.

I can still see Doctor Hélène standing at her desk, her hands folded under her scapula, her face clear of the powder I had noticed the day before. Her manner, as severe as a schoolteacher readying a reprimand, contributed to making her look faded. She readied her performance with a nod in the direction of Father Brabant; then a pause, then a look at the top of her desk, then a look at Mària and me, then a sigh and the words,

"I'm receiving you because it was the father who requested that I do," she said. "Whether by omission or commission, your attendance here has brought disrepute on the Queen Elisabeth Clinic and on its director."

At that, Father Brabant asked that Mària and I wait outside; he wanted to talk to the director alone. We nodded and tapped our chests. Forty years or so after this event, I had collected enough incidents in my life as a nun to conclude that religious rules commanding harmony were unfailingly helpless against immature, selfish, and vain superiors. The at-all-times wise, gentle, and humble mother superior is another convent myth perpetuated by the outside world.

As my notebook must have surmised long ago, the wages of my youth was foolishness. When I first met Doctor Hélène, I thought she was the most confident woman on the planet. It was self-absorption, not confidence, that had reduced the nun to an entitled autocrat, wielding power over a community terrified of contracting Bantu diseases. She had built that entitlement at the expense of her vow, humanity, and Hippocratic oath. A firefighting arsonist was loose here. This will surely beggar the idea readers have of the consecrated life, where harmony, discipline, and sacrifice reign supreme. Those who have read Kathryn Hulme[1]'s novel will not believe what I am reporting here; it is so contradictory. So be it.

---

1.   http://en.wikipedia.org/wiki/Kathryn_Hulme

Exigences of all kinds produced monsters and other creatures resembling Henry Morton Stanley from the beginning of Belgian colonial rule of the middle of Africa. There was, however, no greater exigency in 1945, from the standpoint of Belgian and Bantu, master and servant, than navigating the new colonial living arrangement following the wreckage of World War II.

For over an hour, Mària and I stood in the hall on the third floor of the main clinic, catching up on the devotions we had missed. To our credit, we had no illusion as to the outcome of the discussion going on inside; and we dare not look at each other, preparing our psyche for what was to come. We witnessed our own history unfold before our eyes, and its bitter disappointment weighed heavily upon us. The fact is that history is nothing if not a stutterer. We were not sure what it really had in store for us. All we knew for sure at that moment was that drums were murmuring in the distance. The Bantus were exchanging information. Their whispers echoed through and blended with the sound of large tropical raindrops falling on colonial corrugated tin roofs. Along with those sounds, my friend, the word, who had not harassed me in a long while, decided that the time was propitious to mingle its rhythm with the talking drums of the Bantus and the sound of the tropical rain.

When Father Brabant came out there was no evasion. "Doctor Hélène has agreed to keep you at the clinic only as sisters in transit," he announced. She did not say so to Father Brabant, but the implication was that she would not appeal to the governor to put us on the government payroll at the clinic like the Missionary Franciscan Sisters of Marie.

Mother Melchior met us outside of the clinic. Doctor Hélène had telephoned her the news. Solicitously, she offered that I stay at the Sacred Heart Sisters' Residence until Jerome arrived from Matadi. He would then accompany me to Wembo-Nyama. In exchange, I would not be permitted to go back to the clinic. Instead, I would spend my time in prayer at the Sainte Anne Chapel. The next train to Mària's destination, Kolwezi, 2,036 kilometers from Leopoldville, 1,116 kilometers from Wembo-Nyama was scheduled the following week. The exact day was not yet known. Regardless of the date, no more than seven days remained to us.

I was dazed, my whole body was numbed, and I am still sure after all the intervening years that had I known what future awaited us, I would not have been able to bear life then.

We found a singular comfort in planning how we would reunite. Most of the time, however, we discussed leaving the sisterhood. A letter to Mària's parents asking for the plane tickets to Brussels would get us out of Leopoldville in record time. Mària checked with Sabena Airline for the schedule of their Douglas DC 3s to Brussels, and I found out from the *évolué* at the administrative center how to get a car to take us to the aerodrome. We doubted that anyone would stop us. We would leave a note for when they missed us and came to check. (Yet, when the moment of departure came, we just picked up our bags and got on the train, Mària to Kolwezi; Jerome and I to Wembo-Nyama. Conscience; not our plans had its way with us.) During the time left to us, we lived in fear of jinxing being together again; and we were careful not to say or do anything that would suggest a go-with-God sort of final farewell. That became obsessive to the point that not even making love was exempt from the dread that it would be a last salute to our feelings for each other. Consequently we didn't, one of my five most consequential regrets.

Upon parting we clang to the view that we would be reunited in no more than two years. No sweet farewell, by any means; still, our grief was made bearable by the understanding that we would be together again. All the same, Kolwezi and Wembo-Nyama consummated the rift between the Tournai part of our journey and the Congolese one. All the same too, it took me a long while to face myself; I was existentially adrift without Mària. I was gutted. No Ostend sole was ever gutted as I was. There, I said it without a hint of the guilt that persecuted me for so many years.

Chapter 16

An angel of the Lord in the person of Jerome got off the train in Leopoldville on the morning of October 29, 1945, the same train Mària and I had arrived on just eleven days before. As soon as he had one foot on the platform, he set about helping me endure Mària's departure. There was no question of triumphing over grief. I just sought to endure. Jerome's first words were about her. I was so used to people being enamored with Mària and not me that I didn't even think then that Jerome possibly had come to Leopoldville for her and not for me, his employer. I told him what had happened, as if he were an old friend.

"Sister," he said, "I thought Sister Mària was an angel." Then he said, "Sister, God bonds forever those who love each other."

He said that with an earnestness such that only heaven could have commanded. I accepted his words for divine reassurance, the only time I would take anything as an indication from heaven. If I have lived this long, that sign is responsible. I made a refrain of it and incorporated it into every decade of rosaries I ever recited since. That experience sealed my attachment to Jerome. To his credit he never took advantage of my singular regard for him. It's true that he was full of gratitude for being taken out of his dead-end Matadi existence. He was also full of willingness to do whatever was asked of him. He was one of my most laudable decisions.

We took the train the next day. Mother Melchior had tried to talk me into staying in the Leopoldville area as the bishopric's liaison to the Queen Elisabeth Clinic, but Father Brabant was opposed to an insignificant assignment for me and insisted I take up the duties for which I was trained and had come to the Congo. Wembo-Nyama was moreover a more forthcoming place to wait for Mària than the bottlenecked Leopolville. (Besides Father Brabant was under no illusion about the future of Belgians in the Congo following the war. Leopoldville, the capital, was about to become the center of the inevitable contention between the parties contending for the new post-colonial supremacy.) I had long realized that Mother Melchior's purpose was to separate Mària from me. That achieved, she didn't care where I ended up. In any case, distance from the place of Mària's debacle and mine was all I sought, as quickly as possible.

Father Brabant and Mother Melchior came to the station to see Jerome and me off. Seven months later she visited Wembo-Nyama. Sister Angeline, one of our hospital sisters, reported that when she went to wake her for matins, she was drunk. It seems that, like me, she was a solitary drinker. In 1947, she and bishop Six departed Leopoldville for Brussels, forever out of our lives. Father Brabant became Bishop of Leopoldville soon after.

The journey from Leopoldville to Wembo-Nyama took a little more than two days. In 2000, the trip taking us back to Leopoldville renamed Kinshasa took half that. During the voyage I began to teach Jerome to speak French properly. He could not be an honest *évolué,* I told him, unless he learned to speak correctly. Whether that had any effect, I am not sure. Fifty-five years later when he reminisced on our 1945 journey to Wembo-Nyama his French was still approximate.

Nevertheless by the time we reached our destination he could say both the Pater Noster and Hail Mary in seamless Kikongo accented French. At one point in the journey, however, he recited the Hail Mary in Kikongo, his native language. I was stunned. I wish I knew a word other than lyrical to express the impact the Hail Mary in Kikongo had on me. What I'm saying here hardly does justice to what I heard except that it was in words what Raphael's Mary was in paint. Fortunately, the Trinity had endowed me with the inquisitiveness to make me want to learn that Hail Mary from Jerome. When I finally did, I would recite it slowly, the way Mària and I would sometimes make love, to savor every up, every down, every pause. I haven't said a Hail Mary in my own native tongue since 1945. *O nge vana venakento nkua nsambu yo malau ye mbongo a vumu kiaku Yezu.* I wrote that in one swoop. It gives me courage. It also sort of anchored me to Wembo-Nyama. Since I could never go native, it made me part of the people.

We made countless stops on our meander to Wembo-Nyama. At several stops, Jerome found fresh mangoes for me to satiate my singular fondness for that fruit. Yes, it reminded me of the savor that I loved above all others – Mària. As luck would have it, when we arrived in Wembo-Nyama we found a Jamaican woman among the Methodist missionaries there. Her name was Sister Shirley, a very handsome indefatigable evangelical minister. She had come to Wembo-Nyama carrying the seeds of a certain variety of mango from her homeland. She already had a substantial orchard of trees bearing that priceless fruit, when we arrived. Jerome took a liking to her for the singular mangoes her mission's orchard produced and other reasons I suspect. To obtain these mangoes, high-ranking officials dispatched their drivers from miles away. Sister Shirley called them 'Julie.' She made sure that all our patients had slices of her delicacy for their afternoon snack. So delectable were they, for many it was the highlight of the day. I feasted on Julies unreservedly and kept a few in my room and office for their refined fragrance when ripe.

We penetrated the Congolese countryside as one penetrates a tunnel. All along I looked for Switzerland so that I could commune with Mària through the medium of the geography we dreamed about. The sky was expansive, the landscape vast, and some trees were so massive only the Trinity Himself could have planted them. Nevertheless we did not pass any spot remotely resembling Switzerland's holiday posters. The sight of people breaking into termite edifices in search of food was not for tourists' eyes. Enough of that. Our debacle of the past week had made me more pessimistic, and I was no longer looking for holiday posters.

This is the part I dreaded telling most of all when I began experiencing the yearning to reach out to the outside world with Mària's and my story. Either I have to tell this part of our story reluctantly or I won't be able to tell our story at all. I'm relying on memory mostly, for there are almost no entries in my notebook about this part. I would have preferred to omit it, but there would be no *ontknoping*, unknotting, to our story, otherwise. Here is why.

Mària was in hell, the Sixth Circle to be exact. The one they bury you in a tomb on fire. So it read between the lines of her first letter, which arrived a few weeks after I ensconced in Wembo-Nyama. It was a short one-paragraph letter, a last testament to a loved one. Her pain had metastasized to her spirit. I cannot bring myself to quote what she wrote. Fortunately, I was given permission to use the hospital wireless and the operator was able to reach Father Brabant for me after a few hours. Meanwhile I laid face down on the floor of our chapel, prostrate in prayer. Mària who was terrified of rape had been defiled by men in the village in the vicinity of her institution. An orphanage resident named Alonse guided the men to her. The day before, she had reprimanded him for leading a group of boys in an animal sacrifice of the orphanage's dogs. The men burst into her cabin as she was washing before the evening meal. She was found unconscious, when a sister came looking for her. Alonse and the other boys involved in the sacrifice had fled.

Bishop Six immediately sent an aide, good Monsignor Mercier, to Kolwezi to bring her out. She was now back at the Elisabeth Clinic under the personal care of Mother Sainte-Ursule. "You should be on the next train to the clinic," Father Brabant cried. "She is completely destabilized . . . completely destabilized. . . and not responding to treatment. She only has your name on her delirious lips and something about forgiveness. As soon as she can travel, the bishopric is flying both of you home to Tournai."

This was on a Tuesday, I recall. The train to Leopoldville was scheduled for Friday, which meant that I would not see Mària until Sunday and die a thousand times until then. Didn't Matthew say, *For where your treasure is, there your heart will be also?* I gave Jerome the choice of staying in Wembo-Nyama or of coming with me. I told him what had happened to Mària and said that I preferred he remain in Wembo-Nyama because I would be going back to Belgium when Mària got better. At the time, I didn't think of bringing him to Belgium with me. He chose to come with me to the clinic, to keep me company, he said, and help however he could. When I left for Belgium, he would return to Matadi. He did not care for a construction job in Wembo-Nyama, regardless of my entreaties he do so. On the train we prayed. We did not eat. We did not drink. We prayed.

Father Brabant was at the train station when we got in Sunday morning. It was shocking how much he had aged. Naturally, I assumed it was because of the guilt he was experiencing for mentoring Mària to go to the Congo. However, he also had a measure of a smile on his face. After an apology for sounding unhinged when we spoke on the wireless, he explained that

"Sister Mària has improved. She is siting up and is praying. She has no recollection of the attack. She knows you're coming and said she was grateful for that. I told her about sending the two of you home. A mistake she called that and other things I did not understand."

I could not have imagined then that being told they were sending us home would precipitate what Mària was to do next. Tears smeared her beautiful pale cheeks when I entered her room. She extended her arms. Father Brabant, God bless his soul, asked the sister in the room with her to come out. I was there to sympathize in the Greek sense of the term, "to suffer with" Mària, and there could be no rule against that. We hugged for dear life.

We consoled each other. Then, I remember Mària becoming suddenly focused as if all her senses and intellectual powers were pointing in one single direction. The change was startling, and I recoiled.

"What is it," I asked. "Are you remembering things?"

She looked at me the way she did in the old days when she was about to do something surprising. For a long while she looked at me that way, as if judging what my reaction was going to be. She then said the strangest thing,

"I want to tell you something but I want Father Brabant to hear it too." I knew instinctively she was leaving the sisterhood. She, whose ambition since primary school was to be a nun renunciant, was walking away from the convent. Plus she was not going home.

After Father Brabant had left the room, she told me that she was joining a Kikongo religious commune in Nsanda, a village near Leopoldville she had heard about. That's where *the least of these* were. That's what God had been trying to tell her all this time. Had she listened, she would not have been put through so many blunders. She did not want me with her. She was very clear about that. Father Brabant would not use anything except Mària's own volition to put her on a plane home. I suggested that she be drugged and taken to the aerodrome. He looked at me as if I were out of my mind. Mària's resolve having passed the point of no return, I took the action that reflected my hopelessness: I went back with Jerome to Wembo-Nyama.

Bishop Six had contacted Mària's parents earlier, and they came to Leopoldville within the week and the bishop's driver took them to Nsanda. She told them she was not going with them. To forget her. She was home. They took the train to Wembo-Nyama to commiserate with me and tell me what their daughter said. They blamed Father Brabant. God did they blame him! He was the one, who had rose-colored the Congo for Mària. I reminded them as subtly as I could that no one had a mind of her own like Mària. Wisely, the bishop had not told them she had been raped in Kolwezi. I felt ill the entire time I was with them. They were contorted in pain and incredulity and looked as if they would die. Most of the time we sat silently together looking at the ground in numb incomprehension.

Bishop Six had me come back to Leopoldville three months later to go see Mària. In his Land Rover, Germain, his driver, took me to Nsanda, seventy-eight kilometers south of Leopoldville early in the morning. The dirt road made it a bumpy four-hour drive, and we got there at ten o'clock. Nsanda was an isolated village between the Congo River and its tributary the Kwango. Dust rose from the dry land whenever there was a wind. Rain was not common to these parts. The sky was cloudless and so pale I remember it looked almost white. When we got there, Germain went to speak to an elderly man seating outside a ndako, hut. He came back to the vehicle to tell me that the elder was going to take us where Mària was. As we entered the village's courtyard, I stopped to take long breaths and look around. The village seemed divided into four sets of four bandako. We followed the elder west, to the other side of the village, where stood an old baobab tree. Under the tree, Mària was seated on the ground surrounded by a dozen children of all ages reciting the alphabet in French. When she saw us, she showed no surprise; but told the children to tell us good morning. They did in unison. Their voices broke my heart. I remember that well. Mària was dressed like a village woman, wearing a scarf over her hair and a long Congolese dress that had once been green colored. She stood up with some difficulty, and I thought she was still in pain. It's when she put her hands on her abdomen that I saw she was pregnant. Oh God, I thought mechanically. She dismissed the children; I in turn asked Germain to wait for me in the Land Rover, and I went to her. We embraced long. I sought the scent that I remembered, but it was no longer there.

My very first impression was that she looked content and was where she wanted to be. Other than the pregnancy and the faded dress, she was the same Mària. Her face, as beautiful as ever, was a bit thinner, in spite of the pregnancy, but that was all. The difference was with me. On a day like this, what I felt was made exponentially worse for recalling the joys we had experienced together. After it occurred to me that her descent into hell was complete and there was nothing anyone could do about it now I had an impossible time looking her in the eyes. I struggled to recapture the past, to a time that felt distant. It felt as though I was lost in an infinite ocean, confined in a different existence, a different reality.

"Let's go to my hut," she ordered. "It's cooler there, and by the look of you, more comfortable."

We passed women seated in circles preparing food. Babies on their backs, singing softly, a few were pounding what looked like sweet potato leaves in a wooden mortar. They all greeted Mària casually as if she were one of their own. If it were not for the color of her skin, she would be another village woman. She returned their greetings the same way. As for men, only old ones were around.

From the outside, her hut looked the same as the others. Inside was sparse, a single-sized bed plus a crucifix at the head, a table and a couple of chairs, a blue plastic clothes cabinet with a zipper in the middle. That was all. No light fixture. No running water. The zebra-skin rug on the dirt floor seemed out of place.

One of the women came in with an earthen jar, and Mària told her in French that it was a bit early for that. The woman answered in Kikongo and both she and Mària laughed. I didn't ask what was said.

"This is for you. It's palm wine," Mària said with a chuckle when I sat down. "Will you want lunch?"

I shook my head no, and the woman left.

"Tell me about Wembo-Nyama," Mària said.

"First let me tell you why I am here," I answered. "Bishop Six asked me to come, and I jumped at the chance to see you."

"They won't give up, will they?" she said exasperatedly. "They know that you and Father Brabant are the only people from that community I'll see. Well, you can tell them I'm pregnant. That should turn them off. Obviously Father Brabant didn't tell them. You do it. Tell them too that I now belong to the Church of Jesus Christ on Earth established by the Prophet, Simon Kimbangu[1]. This is his village. "

"Kimbangu?" I said, surprise; remembering what Sister Shirley had told me recently about Kimbanguism. Her Methodist superiors in Britain had heard about the sect and asked the mission in Wembo-Nyama to send a report. Probably because she was black, she was given the task of traveling throughout the Congo and compile a history of what the Methodist Church of Great Britain considered an opposing

---

1.   http://www.britannica.com/eb/article-9045460/Simon-Kimbangu

denomination because Kimbangu followers were establishing programs of community assistance in the south of the Congo and in Leopoldville. Once when we were talking about the difference between her church and mine, she brought up what she had found about Kimbanguism. "It's a new model that makes perfect sense for the Congo," she had said. "It's evangelical with a Congolese flavor. Christianity, à l'africaine."

She thought that Belgium and the church had made a grave blunder in martyring Kimbangu. (In 1960 she too joined the Kimbangu ministry that became the largest in Africa and is now part of the World Council of Churches.)

"Yes, Mària said. Prophet Simon Kimbangu[2], who like Christ performed miracles. Like Christ who was condemned to death by the Roman colonists, he was condemned to death by the Belgian colonists. That was in 1921, the year he came to this village. The abomination in my life I must tell you now was to have believed that the Creator had anointed me with a unique understanding to act in Belgium's name. I have forsaken my family and remain here to serve the people. I do that with a zeal bound in humility. And I care for my own needs and do not rely on the Congolese to serve me as they did before. In Kolwezi I found the true way, and I embraced the Church of Jesus Christ on Earth founded by the Prophet Kimbangu[3]. My brothers and sisters in Kimbanguism succored me, and I found the key that released the shackles of my past as a colonial nun. No one should think for a moment that I came to the Church of Jesus Christ on Earth founded by the Prophet Simon Kimbangu[4] by chance, nor as some reformed alcoholic

2.   http://www.britannica.com/eb/article-9045460/Simon-Kimbangu

3.   http://www.britannica.com/eb/article-9045460/Simon-Kimbangu

colonialist blabbering apologies for white men's crimes in Africa. I joined because it was the true way, having realized that my previous vows were the hypocrisy of my life.

"I am flourishing in my rebirth. That's right, I am flourishing in my rebirth. Remember, 'unless one is born again he cannot see the kingdom of God.' The church I belong to now is my rebirth. Unlike others it does not impose itself on anyone. I commit the gravest of the deadly sins, pride, in saying that my church is as fitting and appropriate as liberation from Belgium will be. It will be a fitting tribute to our future independence. With all the energy God gives me, I work on behalf of both."

All I got out of what she said in that speech was that she had misunderstood the call to become a colonial nun. Was she destroyed because of that misunderstanding? For surely what happened was not what was intended. The consolation for going to the Congo was that she had found rebirth through what she called the true way. I frantically tried to reconnect with her through what she had said. I couldn't succeed. I was too conventional. I couldn't connect with something this weird.

"At least coming to the Congo led you to what you consider the true way," I said. I wanted to talk about other things. Get on firm ground.

"Anybody but you," she said, "I'd think was patronizing me. Was feeling sorry for me."

"Not at all," I said. "If you ask, I'll join you to be with you." I must have sounded sincere, for she said, "You'll always be my love. But this is not a new chapter of our lives. It's a new book."

---

4.   http://www.britannica.com/eb/article-9045460/Simon-Kimbangu

"It certainly is," I said.

For a while we sat just looking at the dirt floor like I did with her parents a couple of months ago in Wembo-Nyama. She was perhaps reflecting on what she was making of what had happened to her, refusing to be a victim, physically and spiritually. I recognized I was in shock, for I kept asking myself the same question: why dear God? I remember too that I was also oddly detached.

From far away, I heard Mària say, "I tell myself that although my guilt for having brought you here is eternal, it's the one contribution I made in my previous life. Nothing can take that away from me." She then burst into tears and putting out her hand in the defensive gesture to keep me from coming to comfort her. "I gave an angel to the Congo," she then said, "maybe that's what God intended. I say this without any false piety."

"What are you talking about?" I asked.

"I know that unlike other Belgians, if you cannot support our Congolese brothers and sisters, at least you will not kill them. You will not be among their killers."

What in the world, I thought.

"Do you mind if I come from time to time to see you?" I asked. "Or if you are able you'll come to Wembo-Nyama."

"Yes, of course," she said.

"Perhaps when the baby is due, you can send me a message and I'll find a way with Father Brabant's help to be here."

"Yes, that would be nice."

We talked on and on for another hour about everything and chuckled uneasily when a recollection was poignant or funny. Then I left, never to see her again.

From Father Brabant I heard that the baby was a girl. From him too I heard that Mària had joined one of the independence movements emerging throughout the Congo faster than the grass of the savannah. Every tribe had a movement. I heard a lot of things from Father Brabant until the news of her death. With time, I thought of her less often. Instead of every minute, she passed through my mind every hour or so. I would have preferred to see her as we were in Tournai and not as she was in the village of Nsanda. For some reason that's how my mind gave her to me.

Chapter 17

It was in 1955. Unlike most of my years in the Congo that are tied together like a bundle of wheat stalks, 1955 stands out clearly because it was the year the dry season began to linger longer than we were used to, stretching until there was no other season.

As I watched the land go from a green forest to a vast savannah, I was amazed and humbled to see that nature, at its most basic, did not develop in a faultless way, as we had been taught. As I saw the landscape transform from forest to savannah, I prayed over it.

The drums were mad with questions, wondering what had offended the drummers' ancestors to withhold for so long the wet season. A feast of beats the drums were, everyone seeming to have an opinion about the wayward rain and wanted to share it. Every session began with two full strokes. "I don't understand," the drummer was announcing.

Bishop Brabant was on his last tour of the season. I knew he had stopped in Wembo-Nyama more to reminisce about Mària than to inspect the hospital and see how the mission was holding up against the Evangelicals, Methodists and what have you. His visit gave me an opportunity to query him more about the daughter Mària had in 1946. She had named her Kolo for Kolongonu, Perfect in Lingala, the wonderful fusion of every language ever spoken in the Congo, from Portuguese to Swahili. Why she had not chosen a French name came to me in a dream. I was impatient to tell the bishop. Kolo was three when Mària died, and Father Brabant tried to get her from the

Nsanda village. He designated an *évolués* to help him. When he told me what he was trying to do, I offered to help with a sum of money to the village's headman. I would get it from the inheritance my uncle had left me. The headman refused, saying that Kolo was a living image of her mother. It would be a desecration to sell her. Later, the *évolués* reported that the villagers sent Kolo "South," possibly to Angola or Zambia to live with Kimbanguists there in case the Mbulamatadis tried to kidnap her.

"I have appeals everywhere for her," Bishop Brabant told me disheartened." I offered to help them get the Kimbangu Church recognized by the World Council of Churches. She has been moved several times, I'm sure. That's all I know. I have pleaded with the village to no avail – "

"You should let her go, father," I interjected. "Mària wants us to let her go. I had this dream: Mària was saying that she gave her daughter a local name because she belonged to the Congo." He was not convinced.

"Then why did she die," he asked. He could never say kill herself. He regarded it as his duty – perhaps penance is a better word – for the blame he felt regarding Mària.

As he was leaving he had a sermon for the staff, which was also his custom. A wonderful speaker, he loved motivational lectures about the Trinity's work in the Congo. The staff responded with fervor to his exhortation and never failed to give him an ovation as he walked to his Land Rover. In 1955, however, he had more than the Trinity's work in mind. He had concerns that native practices were conflicting with the Good News he and others before him had brought to the Congo. I wrote in my notebook that he actually said, "Bantu practices

[were] opposed to the teaching of the Cross." Devotion to masks, he said, was responsible for the void in the soul of the Bantus; keeping them from becoming full-fledged Christians, carriers of the Cross and heaven candidates. When he said that, I looked toward the front pews, where the Congolese staff members were seated. They were listening, outwardly unperturbed by the bishop's denunciation. It was true that most of them were *évolués*, functionaries of the Belgian colonial administration. Seekers of European acceptance, they bought into what Europeans called voodoo practices; and they distanced themselves from their mask-devoted compatriots.

"What was that about?" I asked when it was my turn to say goodbye to the bishop.

"I didn't think you had noticed," was his answer.

"Come on father. Everyone noticed. Your sermons have always been inspirational. Excuse me, but denouncing masks is not inspirational."

"The bishop," he said, "is concerned that when we are no longer running this colony, it will revert to its heathen ways."

I was surprised at his misuse of the third person. His temperament and sense of self did not fit such empty presumption. Had he not also said "heathen," I would have sworn he was joking. I know for sure that Mària would have toned down her zeal for the Congo had he denigrated and not extolled the people when he was mentoring her and me in Tournai.

My constant proximity to the sick and the poor of Wembo-Nyama and the hinterland, the fatalism the Bantus had infected me with, and the fact that I was now thirty-three years old, all combined to make me a bit independent; certainly less tolerant of the rules than when Mària and I set foot in the Congo ten years before. Besides, Bishop Brabant had remained a devoted friend even more so since Mària's death. I could be direct with him with my reactions and questions.

"Has there been a change in church policy, father?" I asked.

He thought for a moment, and, as if taking a dive, he leaped with his answer.

"Like the wet season in these parts," he said, "Belgium's colonization of the Congo is also waning. Until now, the mention of independence was an offense punishable by imprisonment. Now everyone, Belgians and Bantus, speak of independence in no uncertain terms. The notion of Congolese self-determination has become part of the landscape and will never be considered a seditious offense again. What is the church to do?"

(As I relate this episode propped up on Jerome's pillows, I am saying aloud in fear, Dear God, why didn't you gift my dear friend and your dedicated servant 20/20 hindsight so that he could have realized he was pronouncing his own execution. If you had given him that, perhaps he would not have had to do what he did.)

"What is the church going to do," I asked with trepidation, hearing Mària say, "If you cannot support our Congolese brothers and sisters, at least you will not harm them. You will not be among their killers." Dread crept into my heart like that killer disease from upriver that was bewildering us. True enough, Belgium's colonial prospect in the Congo following the Second World War was dimming; maybe my friend like many Mbulamatadis in the Congo was acquiescing to the nihilistic view of destroying what they could not retain. The French did that when the people of Guinea rejected them.

I remember Mària talking passionately about the liberation of the Congo from Belgium at our reunion in Nsanda, and saying that she would do all in her power to see it fulfilled. Liberation, independence, self-determination, whatever name was given to the movements to separate Belgium from the Congo permeated everything everyone did in Wembo-Nyama for the next five years. I was a spectator with a front view of what unfolded. I must say too that I felt an obligation to look at the independence the Congolese sought not with Mària's eyes totally but with the desire that the side she had been on would come out victorious.

The Second World War had brought water to the mill of revolution in colonies everywhere. From Asia to Africa the colonial world was abuzz with change. Before the war, Belgian colonists, the Mbulamatadis, concerned themselves with the climate, their club, which cut of meat was most appropriate at what reception and, of course, how best to protect themselves against Bantu diseases. Life in the colony was simple then. Subsequently I watched the unraveling take place, the blissful illusion dissipate, the specific time when it all changed, and the end coming on the galloping pale horse.

Before I left Tournai following the departure of the German troops, I had a prelude to what relations between Belgians and Africans would be. The *sales boches*, the dirty Germans, had turned Belgium on end. As to Africans living in Belgium, the people sheepishly adjusted how they treated them. It took me a very long time to figure out why. It was simple really: the Germans were responsible. The *sales boches* had done something for Belgium: they had treated Belgians the way Belgians treated Africans. The master race had in effect told Belgians they were no better than the Africans. How could they have done such a thing? Weren't Deutsch and Dutch twins? The disillusionment that ensued could've been enough to cause the additional suicides in the Ardennes Forest, offerings to the master race's perspicacity or lack thereof? The generation that experienced the master race treating Belgians like Africans never recovered from the humiliation. In my collection of clichés about God, there are several about puzzling phenomena and elegies on justice. I'm, however, still searching for a pithy one; so pithy, it will tie Belgians and Africans with a tidy German knot.

Myself, I had little say regarding colonial matters. Prayer and being philosophical about events took the place of any direct involvement I might have had. I was part of it, however, and was interested beyond words in the conclusion. When there were breaks; when I was between patients, and at night, I filled my notebooks with what I saw, sensed and understood from patients, especially the ones connected to independence movements suffering from sleeping sickness, who chatted deliriously during the meningoencephalic phase of the illness. I would tell myself that perhaps it was what the Most High intended, sending me here to be a witness and attest that dominion over others was a sin against His teaching of love of one another.

The Second World War had intruded on colonization like a death knell, and the Mbulamatadis didn't know what to do.

"What would the next chapter have in store for us?" was their ubiquitous question, as stinging as insects in the rainy season. I became sick of hearing Belgians say, *"Nous, pauvres colons"* we poor settlers, as if that were the Brabançonne, the Belgian national anthem. Those who thought that life was made meaningful by reigning over the middle of the Dark Continent were hit especially hard. Before the war, they had their way with the Bantus. Afterwards, they recited verses from the Bible, especially this one from Genesis: 'Perhaps they will hate us and return to us the evil that we have done unto them.' (I heard with my own ears the wife of a colonial officer tell her husband that in our chapel.) No bad conscience ever haunted dreams the way Belgian dreams were haunted in the Congo. In order to exorcise the spirit of wrongs from their colonial past, they initiated campaigns of praise to all that the Mbulamatadis had brought the Congolese.

The Bantus, however, had none of it; and as the decade of the '60s approached, even the *évolués* felt shame for what had been inflicted on them. They were like rape victims. Colonization would forever stain their soul. When disenchantment sets in, there is no way to recapture the moment. You have to start all over again. Mbulamatadis, however, did not care to start over. They dug in, insisting that the old master servant ways be maintained at all cost with a measure of paternalism for those so inclined.

The Bantus, I think, resented our attempt at being parents to them more than they did Leopold's brutality toward their fathers. There is a certain sharpness to brutality that leaves no room for ambiguity regarding the position of the ones who have been subjected to it. Brutality is predictable. Paternalism was something else. It had the Bantus wondering what we would subject them to next. That made them restless and guarded.

The Mbulamatadis responded with disjointed colonial policies. By then, they had as much credibility as the dunce who challenges reason. The post-war policies became contortion exercises, as the Mbulamatadis didn't know which way to turn as they groped to maintain control of the colony. Violence became a familiar companion, growing alongside the dehumanization that had taken hold long ago. The Mbulamatadis were determined to exact retribution upon the Bantus for daring to challenge their authority. They became consumed by a fervor to dehumanize the Bantus, in order to curse and accuse them of all evils, all in the name of maintaining their power. Practicality should have inhibited these behaviors, but it did not. Colonialism is an ideology that stands alone, depicting the brutal reality of human brutality toward one another, fueled by arrogance and the dehumanization of others.

To be sure, most of the colonialists were – God forgive me – lowbrow, petit bourgeois at best, Mària's nemesis. "Petit bourgeois are loath to accept their inferior position in society; so they search for others to place beneath them," Mària had adjudged. An African colony was the perfect venue for the petit bourgeois to practice placing others beneath them. Whenever I came across one who reeked of having come to the Congo for that purpose, I rebuked him unreservedly, as Mària would. I made a conscious effort to suppress my desire to imitate Mària, my tendency to be overly critical, and my obligation to the Trinity. It was important to remember that, while it may be perverse, the universal trait of having inferiors is a common human characteristic.

I witnessed this, but as I said earlier, I had little involvement in colonial matters. I was a hospital nurse and administrator concerned with patients' health. Nevertheless I sought to mitigate our dominion over the Bantus by providing the best service humanly possible to the patients and the people of the Wembo-Nyama region. The reactionaries among my colleagues accused me of seeking to displace the Madonna in the Order of the Bleeding Heart. Their malicious reproach did not affect me, for until 1955 at least, I had the full support of Bishop Brabant. (When independence came to the Congo, others ran for their lives, chased out of the Congo by the arisen Bantus. In Wembo-Nyama, where we were even more at their mercy, it was just another day. That was not due to practicality for the Bantus were not a practical people. It was our ministration – our willing ministration – of the people there that made the difference.

Undoubtedly, colonization would have been more successful had it been in the form envisioned by Leopold II, personal and direct. Leopold, however, unleashed such evil on the Congo that colonization had to be appropriated by the state and turned into an industrial complex. Belgians and other Europeans derived their empire from those colonial industrial complexes; and in their rut to possess African land created misdesigned unpronounceable borders to curse the Bantus with and remind them that Mbulamatadis had passed this way. The borders are witness to colonization's truth to have created a new world. People who do not fear God are like people who do not fear death. They are ruthless. In the case of Belgium, the Second World War erased all notions the Bantus might have had that Belgium was invincible. Thus alerted as if by a spirit, the Bantus awoke to the conviction that every facet of colonization, including the church, was the source of their misery. Suddenly, they became aggressive and irredentist. With horrific consequences, it was their turn to fall all over themselves to take advantage of Belgium's diminished stature. As befitting a people with a great sense of oral tradition, the shadow of the past was never far from the present. It was as if every Bantu was standing watch over a grave, waiting for his painful colonial memories to rise up.

Bishop Brabant told me, "I think that even if Belgium can't control this colony physically, it can still do so spiritually. Isn't that the most important thing? But for that to happen, we have to separate the Bantus from their pagan ways of worship. We need to make it more likely that they will follow the church. I hear that you favor these people. That's fine; but I would think that, as a medical person, you'd be eager for them to learn that microbes and what have you cause diseases and not local mask-wearing witchdoctors."

That was the last thing he ever said to me. I never I saw him again.

Later that year, he answered his own challenge and went in person to a Ngbandi village near the border with Ubangi-Shari (present day Central African Republic) reputed for its use of masks in ancestors and animistic religious practices. The Ngbandi people raised their children to be warriors and had taken to the church grudgingly. On arrival in that village, he was given palm wine as tradition commanded. The wine was spoiled. His aide, who drank the wine too, became sick also. Delirious, the bishop gave an impromptu sermon, expressing regret for what he had come to do to the village. The chief, in all appearance satisfied, put him and the aide in a hut to recover. The investigators reported that when the day was at its hottest, and the villagers were in their huts hiding from the midday sun, the bishop must have walked to the nearest riverbank and waded into the water. Only pygmy chimps in the treetops were witness to his final moment. His body was found two days later on the bank of one of the islands in the middle of the Ubangi River. His hands were clasped in prayer.

I told myself that whatever the tale of Mària's life and mine and Father Brabant's among the Bantus was it would be an allegory for all the rivers in the Congo. Rivers that meander uncoiled and placid to entice presumptuous European missionaries to their shores to ensnare them; then to suffocate them with boa constrictor-like curls as lethal as a hangman's noose.

Epilogue

To my amazement, the Congo became independent in May 1960. History defeated the colonial protagonists, and without the Congolese comprehending how.

In 1959 Brussels officially recognized Mària's church, the Church of Jesus Christ on Earth established by the Prophet, Simon Kimbangu[1]. It was already too late; no about face could have saved Belgium's colonial venture in Africa. The Bantus no longer saw us. We were history's ghosts. As if they were witnessing God's punishment for our having been presumptuous to assume we were His instruments, marching hand in hand with Him as friends, doing His will, they now laughed at us. Instead of laughing at us, I wish they had appreciated what was about to befall them. For fatalists, they were remarkably optimistic that independence would initiate a golden age in the Congo. Liberation exerted a gravitational pull, irresistible – malicious in many ways. The Congolese were eager for a new day, any new day. I was in the whirlwind, watching decolonization give the Congo a wild ride. People who had no idea what it was about joined the bandwagon. Would they have done so knowing it was for their own funeral, for within days, the new country turned against itself. As if an evil had infected it, the people cracked along ethnic lines. Mària would have been horrified. She had to have known, and that, in my view, is the main reason she killed herself

---

1. http://www.britannica.com/eb/article-9045460/Simon-Kimbangu

When independence struck, many Belgians including prelates fled, surprise on their faces, mobs at their heels, bats and machetes held high. I thought of leaving too as rumors that the new Prime Minister, Patrice Lumumba, had communist tendencies and was associated with the faithless Soviet Union. That, however, was momentary. Mària had died here. I told myself it would be a betrayal if I left without a second thought. Besides, as a medical nun I appreciated that illnesses knew no dominion, colonial or otherwise. With all my heart, I came to believe that being in the Congo and healing the people was proof that I was doing the Trinity's will. I insisted on separating myself from my country's colonial venture in the Congo. Then too I stayed because the new authority in Wembo-Nyama asked my order to keep me in place. I had treated many of its members, and when they approached us, they did so with no pretense they knew how to run a hospital for the poor. Auxiliary Bishop Joseph-Albert Malula had hoped that I would stay, and I couldn't say no to someone whose views of what the Congolese church should be were so similar to Mària's. A Bantu, Bishop Malula created the Congo Rite, a Congolese liturgy. He was made archbishop of Leopoldville in 1964 if memory serves. His Holiness Paul VI then made him cardinal five years later. He asked that I accompany him to the Vatican for the ceremony of investiture, and I went. There was also the simple fact that no one was as proficient in treating trypanosomiasis, sleeping sickness, as I had become. Treatment with arsenic was effective but necessitated an expert's hand to administer drugs like melarsoprol. A traditional nun by default, one cast in error, I became a star in my role as a medicine provider. That alone would have kept me at my hospital in Wembo-Nyama if only to train a Bantu staff and the others who came from various parts of Africa to learn from us. I was needed. Blessed are the needed is similar to blessed are those who love much.

There were also challenging illnesses like the one from people who had killed chimps for bush meat. Nothing about this pathogen made sense. It began with a cough and ended with cancers. Those infected suffered a hundred percent death rate. Travelers coming from southeastern Cameroon on the big river spread it through the unimaginable number of prostitutes in the new urban centers. Bantus were sure this was another Mbulamatadis scheme to deny them independence. Those were the crucible years I thought would never end. Time was so hectic, it was a sort of comfort whenever I remembered to feel sorry for myself.

These memories have deepened my end-of-life interlude. They have also prompted me to ask, why wait for memories? Blessed is she who grasps her present with both hands and leaves no room for memories or regrets.

My head on Jerome's pillows I smile at the ceiling. I love the sound of the rain on the roof. My smile is also to deride all the efforts to castoff our nature. Neither bound breasts, nor convents' ramparts kept desire at bay. Rules cannot invalidate the self, meanness, or any of the other characteristics we are saddled with. Blessed is she, however, who is burdened with love.

On every anniversary of her leaving on May 12, 1948, Mària, now a rainmaker, waits by the outside-of-time gate for when I decide to join her. In the background, Miles Davis is playing in a grove of palm trees. That, in addition to the rain, friends, is ample reason to make her wait no longer.

"Octopus of mine, why did I do what I did, you think?" she will ask when I step through. I've thought about that since 1948 and I'll be ready.

"You acted in accordance with your nature," I'll say. "It's not because you were suffering from any white skin black African mask syndrome." Absolutely not! What you went through was more profound than that. You saw the circumstances afflicting the Bantus and your nature directed you to champion them. At least that's what I think. You were presumptuous, sure; but you were wired that way. However, after having reflected all these years on why you did what you did, I concluded that you perceived that you would fail; that there was no hope for them; that the Congo would be the most wretched country in the world as far as time could cover. You were blinded by the exigencies your nature imposed on you. What happened to us had probably weakened you more and you had no strength left to fight back. So you had one of your monstrous climaxes, a real crescendo of pessimism; and you gave full reign to your self-centered nature and it ditched it all for you, including your inside-of-time life."

"We have a while to discuss my nature," she will say, laughing. "Let's listen to Miles welcome you. I told him *That Old Black Magic* was one of your favorites, and he's been rehearsing ever since you entered that awful nursing home."

Suicide is like blessed solitude, the purveyor of freedom. Later this evening it will help me go to sleep to the sound of the rain on the roof. I will bless my closed left fist with a kiss, before swallowing its melarsoprol content that's full of an arsenic organic compound. I will chase the melarsoprol with a few satisfying swigs of cassava-roots brandy that I brought from Wembo-Nyama. I will then pick up the piece of rope made of interwoven sisal that I found on the ship that ferried Mària and me to the Congo from Antwerp back in 1945. I have slept with it since 1948. As you can imagine, I thought of using it as Mària had. I had concerns, though, that my significant weight loss might not be sufficient for a successful procedure. Lightly I will pass through the neutral zone there between the inside and the outside-of-time gates.

I smile at what the orderly, who didn't know there was a place called the Congo – a dunce if ever there was one – will say. He will cackle when he finds me in the morning: "*La Folle de Tournai* is as cold as a prison door and holding a piece of rope in her left hand." My story will then be told. May yours be as rewarding.

Thanks for taking the time to read this. If you liked this book, it would mean a lot if you could take a moment to leave a review on your favorite online store. Thanks so much!

ALSO BY CHRISTIAN FILOSTRAT

Frantz Fanon in the U.S.A., followed by comments from Fanon's wife
Negritude and its Revolution
Containing China
The Secret of the Dictator
Until You, Who